A ROBE OF FEATHERS

a robe of feathers

AND OTHER STORIES

Thersa Matsuura

COUNTERPOINT · BERKELEY

Library of Congress Cataloging-in-Publication Data

Matsuura, Thersa.
A robe of feathers and other stories / Thersa Matsuura.
p. cm.
1. Japan—Fiction. I. Title.
PS3613.A8415R63 2009
813'.6—dc22
2008051520

ISBN 978-1-58243-489-6

Cover design by Gopa & Ted2
Printed in the United States of America

COUNTERPOINT
2117 Fourth Street, Suite D
Berkeley, CA 94710

www.counterpointpress.com
Distributed by Publishers Group West

10 9 8 7 6 5 4 3 2 1

Contents

A Robe of Feathers   3

Hate and Where It Breeds   12

The Bean Washer   17

Yaichiro's Battle   28

Sand Walls, Paper Doors   33

Her Favorite   43

What the Cat Knew   52

Taro's Task   61

One Thousand Stitches   75

Mrs. Misaki's Eyes   80

Devils Outside   92

Tip of the Nose   106

Eden on the 18th Floor   115

The Seed of the Mistake   131

My Devil's Gate   138

Ganguro and the Mountain Witch   151

The Smallest Unit of Time   174

A Robe of Feathers

a robe of feathers

"*Mukashi, mukashi*," the old man began. "There once lived a boy, the youngest of nine children born to parents who, by the time he came along, were both weary and bent from far too many years spent ankle deep in watery rice fields.

The boy was of handsome face and inviting smile but with none of the fine qualities desired in a child. He was not sturdy or brisk like his brothers, not of lively wit or suffering loyalty like his sisters. In fact, the boy tended to burn when he helped in the fields and dream when he worked in the shade.

And so it was decided, as was often done back then, to send the boy to live with a childless couple who had plenty to eat and not enough mouths.

It wasn't long, though, before the boy grew lost there as well and left the house to seek his fortunes elsewhere."

≈

"He's not telling that right," Mother whispered.

"I've heard a thousand versions of this story since I was a child, and I couldn't tell you which one is true." Father rethought that. "Which one is the original, that is."

"I guess you're right," Mother replied, signaling for them to return their ears to the thin sliding *fusuma* door of their son's room.

≈

"Owing to the day's and night's continued warmth the boy was able to find comfort on the black sands of Miho Beach. Gathering the needles from the giant pines, he made a fragrant pillow, which together with the hush and roll of the sea allowed him several years of the most magnificent sleep he had ever had.

"However, one night when he was near eighteen his dreams roamed in sandalwood and giggling tickled behind his ear. When he awoke in the electric blue of predawn, he discovered flapping above his head, hanging from a low, wind-crooked pine branch, a glorious robe made entirely of otherworldly feathers.

"But it wasn't only the perfume that dizzied the boy. Soon after wiping the blur of lingering sleep from his eyes, he realized that while he could still see the white crush of the surf on the sands and observe the seagulls as they dipped and shot sideways in their play, there was only one sound that reached his ears: the coy splash and slap of the woman bathing in the water below."

≈

"When's the last time they've eaten?" Father asked.

"Last night. I've tried everything to get them to come out. Grilled salmon and *miso* soup for breakfast, curry for lunch. Nothing."

"Well, they have to go to the bathroom."

"They do. In turns. Hiro installed a hook-and-eye lock on the door and one stands guard while the other goes. I'm getting worried."

"Ehhh, they'll be fine. They'll get hungry enough, they'll come out. Bet you they're out of there before the end of the day."

"This might have something to do with Grandfather; he's been acting strange recently." Mother moved back away from the door motioning for her husband to follow.

"What now?"

"When you're at work he goes out for walks and doesn't return for hours on end." Mother crossed her arms as if chilled. "He takes bags of bread with him."

"Maybe he's feeding the koi down at the lake. All the old people feed the carp. Doesn't sound strange to me."

"Yeah, that's what I thought, but when I asked him he said it was for the pigeons."

"So he's feeding the pigeons then."

"He told me he was training them," Mother added.

"The man's eighty-four years old, he's got a hobby. We should be thrilled." Father dismissed Mother with a wave of his hand and started down the hall.

"Also, when he is home, before he locks himself up in there with Hiro," Mother tried again, "he just sits at the *butsudan* and talks to Grandmother. It sounds like he's having conversations or something."

"He's lonely. Give the old man a break." Father was already at the *genkan*, pulling on his shoes. "I'm going to pachinko."

Mother gave up as she usually did and returned to her eavesdropping.

≈

"It was the woman in the water who had removed all the sound from the boy's ears, abandoned her only garment on a branch and tiptoed into the ocean to bathe under Mount Fuji."

"Naked?" Hiro stopped his work to look at his grandfather.

"Naked as the day she was—," the old man clucked his tongue. "Angels aren't born, my child." He made a curvy motion with his hands. "They just go around that way." They both laughed.

Hiro knew the woman in the story was an angel. That part never changed, nor did the descriptions of her beauty. Sometimes Grandfather would go on about the creature's upper lip or the high arch of her foot for a good forty minutes or more.

"That's looking mighty fine there, Hiro." The old man slapped the bicycle on the seat. The gentle pat was enough to vibrate the two-dozen lengths of wire secured randomly along the frame, shimmy up their corkscrewed shapes, and release in a cheerful jiggle the twenty-four hard vinyl figures that were attached to their ends. Kamen Rider X, Black, and Amazon all bobbed in perfect unison as if agreeing to the remark about the bike's beauty.

Hiro nodded in time with his action figure friends. The bicycle had come yesterday in the mail. It was the type the old ladies in the neighborhood preferred—three wheels, two on the back with a deep basket in between, a basket on the handlebars as well. He had to special order the color. Old women who gathered in front of the fish market to compare the sparkle in a dead smelt-whiting's eyes only rode black. He debated a mountain bike, they looked nicer, but then he couldn't carry a passenger as easily.

≈

"Damn car won't start." Father was back.

"Shh, what?"

"What did you do to the car? It won't even turn over."

"I went to the store yesterday and it was fine." Mother was again backing away from the door, trying to get her husband to follow.

"Well, it's not fine now. I haven't missed a Saturday afternoon pachinko in years and I'm not about to start today."

"Quiet. They'll hear you."

"Excellent idea." Father began to pull on the door until it rattled in its tracks. "I can borrow that new bicycle to get there." He pulled harder.

"Stop. I told you it's locked. Here, let me look at the car. Maybe I can fix it."

Father grumbled to himself and followed Mother to the front door.

≈

"Cut it out! We're not hungry," Hiro yelled.

Both Hiro and his grandfather were standing on either side of the bicycle, hands planted firmly on their hips, admiring.

"A work of art," Hiro's grandfather said.

"You think so?" Hiro had to admit it was a beauty. "Do you think she'll like it?"

"How couldn't she?"

Hiro spent most of his life not being enthusiastic about anything at all. But recently things had changed. For the first time ever, Hiro was in love. He had a girlfriend. Most people have crushes, fall in love, and date dozens of times before they're thirty-five. But like a pressure relief valve that checks the danger in a pump, he believed this kind of love only dwindled the overall feeling. Hiro had been saving up. He had no doubt that no one had ever known a love as enormous and all-encompassing as the one he felt.

Her name was Mami. She came into the Manga coffee shop on Friday afternoons to sip sugared tea and read two hours' worth of comics. He knew everything there was to know about her. Where she worked, lived, and bought her groceries. He knew she liked chilling her chocolate Poki sticks in a tall glass of iced Fanta—grape flavor—and that she tried to eat fermented *natto* for her health but a few containers, the expiration dates passed, invariably ended up in her garbage on trash day. He even knew that she went to bed at 10:30 every night except Wednesdays when she stayed up to watch a Kimutaka drama.

"Now to get the lights to work." Hiro sat down beside a box full of Christmas lights and began snipping off the plugs with wire cutters. "So this angel chick was nude?"

"Hiro, have some respect." Grandfather settled into the mess on the floor. "The angel was of a beauty incomparable on earth. Her hair so black it shone blue. Her skin, the smooth it had, the sheen of the most flawless pearl.

"The boy knew that she could not fly home without her robe of feathers. He also knew that a celestial nymph's powers fell short of influencing a person's will. If he chose to keep the robe, she could not take it from him. And so he wrapped the warm feathers tightly around his shoulders, even imagining that they clung a little of their own accord, and he was reassured of his choice."

"His choice?" Up until now the story had always ended with the boy stealing the robe. There was never any choice.

"Yes, the boy strode down the beach to retrieve his bride."

"There!" Hiro declared. "It all seems to work now. Ready for a test ride?"

"You betcha!"

"We should probably change first." Hiro removed two hangers from his closet, handing one to the old man. "So, did that guy in the story end up marrying the angel? Did they live happily ever after?"

"Yes, he did. And yes, they did." Grandfather zipped up his trousers and paused. "Until . . ."

"Until?"

"One day she found where he had hidden the robe. By then the boy loved her too much to keep it from her."

"She flew home?"

"Yep. Yep she did." Grandfather pulled on his dress shirt. "What color tie will we be wearing today?"

"Here, I made these last night."

"Pure genius!"

"It's her favorite," Hiro said.

The two finished dressing and Hiro placed a soft pillow in the back basket and helped his grandfather inside.

"Ready?"

"Ready!" Grandfather said. "Don't forget the bread."

≈

The hood was up and Father was cursing so excessively that neither he nor Mother heard the clanking emerging from the side door and move slowly across the gravel to the street.

"Who would steal it? Why?" Father slammed the hood back down, furious. "That's it. I'm going to get the bike."

But before he moved from where he was standing, a commotion erupted a few doors down. Both Mother and Father ran to see what was going on.

"A *decochari*!" someone screamed. "A decoration bicycle!"

"Isn't that the fad in Tokyo?" Mother overheard another voice say.

"I've only read about them in comic books."

Already a handful of curious pedestrians had gathered behind Hiro and his grandfather. They all trotted to keep up with the bright red, three-wheeled bike, a thirty-five-year-old overweight and balding man driving and a sprig thin eighty-four-year-old man squatting in the back basket, enthusiastically massaging a bag of dinner rolls. Periodically one or the other would wave and entice the crowd.

A car battery had been pushed deep inside the front basket. A set of frayed wires attached it to a radio/cassette player taped securely to the handlebars. The song *"Kimi ga Inai Natsu"* ("The Summer Without You"), by Deen, boomed from the black tinny speakers. It was Mami's favorite song. Another set of wires twisted into a long string of Christmas lights, loosely snaking and looping around the two riders.

"Ima wa tooi yasashi kimi wo," Hiro sang loudly, occasionally punching the air with his fist for emphasis. Behind him, Grandfather swayed completely out of time to the music. They both twinkled on and off a festive red, green, yellow and blue.

The two men were a fast-beating rainbow heart inside a monstrous sea urchin on wheels. The animal's quills—the stiff twisted wire—undulating in friendly salute. Newcomers to the crowd couldn't help but gasp.

Mother noticed right away that they were both wearing their formal suits, the expensive black ones that could be used for weddings as well as funerals—all you had to do was replace the white tie for a black one. Today the two wore ties made of daisy chains. Grandfather's whipped up and dropped over his shoulder, dangling down his back. The only thought in Mother's head was her hope that they would not dirty the cuffs of their pantslegs. She watched and followed as they headed towards Miho Beach with what Mother guessed was at least thirty spectators jogging close behind.

Over the road, the twisted pine branches from Grandfather's tale stretched and drooped tufts of prickly green needles. Today they webbed black against the rose-colored setting sun. Naked of any magical cloth, instead they held hundreds of small round shapes, seemingly asleep.

The old man reached into his bag and with one smooth motion flung a handful of breadcrumbs into the air above his head. All at once each shape took flight, each wing up and then down, a quick-beat *whup-whup-whup*, but the image was slower. A net being tossed to the sea, a warm blanket of worn silk. Almost, a robe of feathers.

"Oh, Grandfather. They're beautiful!" Hiro yelled over his shoulder.

The noisy sea urchin approached a traffic light, causing cars to swerve, then slow, then stop. The two men and their flock rode around and around the intersection in large circles. Their growing audience gathered here and there making somewhat of a ring around the show. Young couples held their cell phones up to take pictures of the event, pet owners stayed their dogs, and aproned housewives called to their small children who still galloped close behind the bike, kicking and jumping and spinning.

"Watch this!" the old man called to his grandson. "Cuban Eight!" He readied another fist of crumbs. "Go!" In perfect unison the birds beat their wings twice, went into a figure eight, flipped in midair, and returned to their normal flying position behind the decoration bicycle.

The crowd cheered, applauded. Mother cupped a hand over her mouth.

"What do they think they're doing?" Father demanded.

Hiro looked back at the air show and grinned. "Oh, Mami's going to love it!"

"You haven't seen anything yet." Grandfather said.

The old man was adjusting himself in the basket when the bread bag caught on a particularly bouncy figure of Gamera and spilled onto the street. A hundred pigeons all dove at once, momentarily blinding Hiro.

Seven seconds earlier a man in a small car also could not see. Stuck in the unmoving lane he hit his steering wheel; he was late and didn't understand why the traffic wasn't moving. He drove up onto the sidewalk and with the heel of his hand hard on the horn, sped fast around the other vehicles toward the intersection. The crowd parted for him. The children were quick enough to flee.

Hiro continued his circling, having just enough time to think that the brief moment inside the beating wings felt like a nice place to take Mami on a first date. But longer than that, longer than the anger of the horn, and the moment when everyone seemingly inhaled at once, was the screech of hot tires on cement followed by a silence; and somewhere not far away the soft crush of waves of sand, the call of seagulls at play.

Mother never worried or cared what happened to those two expensive suits and Father never made it to his Saturday afternoon pachinko. Saddest of all maybe was Mami, still two blocks away. She would spend her entire life never marrying, never even imagining that someone could love her as much as Hiro did.

Sixty-two versions of the story would be told by eyewitnesses. There would be other tales, too, by people who came afterwards and children who grew up to remember events differently. But the legend that was told the most, the one that would survive the longest, was the most beautiful one, the one that ended with a tight triangle of birds performing a perfect Aileron roll and carrying a twinkle of colored lights over the sand and sea and into a darkening sky, an angel of sorts flying home. This was the story told by Hiro's Mother.

hate and where it breeds

"I think it might be infected." The boy with the foot-high, baby blue Mohawk carefully wiggled his gold nose ring, winced and shook his hand as if that might relieve the pain.

Just then the train doors swished opened and a greedy snarl of people and things pushed into the car. Once inside the magic touch of bromo-blue light, or maybe it was the Freon-chilled air, saw the knot untangle and disperse.

The Mohawked-teenager never tired of the types that rode the midnight train. In fact, he loved them all. He stood watching wordlessly as a large pair of tangy, musk-smelling tanuki scampered onto an empty two-seater bench and claimed it as their own. In also hurried an entire family of quick chattering *kappa*. Wet and not without slime they made their way to the center aisle and squatted in a tight circle on the floor, their indecipherable conversation and boorish behavior ever-escalating. This greatly distressed the tiny old Bean Washer who couldn't pass to the quieter side of the car and, being too shy to confront the water imps, proceeded to pace back and forth and mumble to himself.

The gaggle of *kappa*, though, caused little trouble for the *tenjo sagari*. A lanky, long-limbed creature that normally resides in the ceilings of Japanese-style houses, it calmly carried its wooly self between two hanging signs and dangled upside down. To the disgruntlement of its father, the inverted creature then proceeded to tickle the youngest *kappa* with its mane of long hair.

The extended shrill of the conductor's whistle cut the air, warning that the doors were about to close. Mohawk-boy stared at what he thought was the last passenger to board the train—a tall, straight-backed, and crimson-faced *tengu*. They almost never came down from the mountains anymore. What a treat!

The creature's grim mouth was turned down into an unmoving scowl; still, you could make out a deep-voiced rumble of murmured prayers and feel the magic they invoked. The Buddhist sutras together with the wooden *clomp-clomp* of the *tengu*'s high, single-toothed *geta* shoes alerted the other passengers he was approaching and in respect—or fear of his legendary temper—every human and beast inside the late-night train ceased their talking and dropped their gaze as he passed. Even the flatulent *kappa* hushed and bowed their saucer-shaped, water-filled heads. The boy watched mesmerized. He noted the tengu's broad back with its massive wings folding and gently twitching. Its long nose was pointing up, and a dreamy fragrance wafted from the mountain goblin's heavy, embroidered robes. *A smell of deep caves, waxy ambergris, and trickery*, the boy thought.

Beside him the train doors were closing when there was a sudden thump, a struggle, and a pained yowl. The boy turned in time to see a businessman wrestle and kick the sliding doors apart and come stumbling into the train. The man carried a soft briefcase in one hand and a copy of the *Japan Times* rolled up in the other. Mohawk-boy noticed the unmistakable peel-off tin tops of two One-Cup-Sakes peeking from both pockets of the man's rumpled suit. He felt a sour twinge of nostalgia.

As a child it was the nightly routine: him fighting his impending bedtime, his mother's weak insistence, followed eventually by the roar of his father.

"Urusai!" he'd yell at both of them.

"I've got an important job for the boy to do," he'd say. "Get over here."

With shiny red cheeks and watery eyes his old man would then fill his palm with loose change and send him down the block to the line of vending machines.

They sold everything there, sodas and teas, rice and batteries. There was even a machine that sold magazines with black sleeves over the covers and beside it a sticky-looking padlocked canister to dispose of them when the reader had finished. Gathering his courage, he'd duck into the bug-filled lights and buy a single One-Cup-Sake and a pack of smokes for his father. He always made sure he received a few extra coins and would treat himself to a can of hot cocoa or red bean soup.

Old Mrs. Kobayashi lived upstairs. Sometimes she'd lean out her bedroom window to chat for a few minutes. "*Otousan* running low, huh?" she'd always ask.

Once home he'd watch the smile spread over his dad's face as he peeled away the top, tossed it aside and drunk the water-clear sake from the thick glass cup. Mother saved those cups. She said they were the only ones the children couldn't break, no matter what they did to them. It was many years later that Mohawk-boy learned milk wasn't supposed to have a slightly alcoholic aftertaste.

The businessman teetered towards the only empty seat, bowing slightly to the Haunted Parasol before sitting down. There was a reason that seat was left vacant. The umbrella-shaped creature continued to swing its single, chubby, frightfully hairy leg back and forth, leaning slightly over to ogle this new passenger with its one unblinking eye. The businessman recoiled as best as he could, but had a hard time escaping the viscous drool that leaked from the creature's lolling tongue. It dampened his knee.

"Doesn't look good." Now that the train was moving again Mohawk-boy's friend was able to continue their conversation. He moved forward, examining the hoop and made a face. Pulling back in what looked like disgust, he ran his hand over his bald head. A tattoo that resembled shattered glass covered most of the left side. It was quite realistic, done in black with red where the blood ran. There were even white highlights to make it look as 3-D as possible. The boy was very proud of that tattoo. He spent an entire semester at the community college designing it himself.

"That's new," Tattoo-boy was trying to read his friend's ripped T-shirt. "B-o-l . . ."

"Bollocks," Mohawk-boy said.

"Yeah, what does that mean anyway?"

"I don't know. I looked it up last night, but it wasn't in my English/Japanese dictionary." He fingered the bold black letters. "Sounds cool though, huh?"

His friend nodded, glancing over to the *kappa*. One had grabbed a handful of the *tenjo sagari*'s hair and was attempting to climb. Two others, most likely the parents, were trying to pull it off while the rest rolled up and down the aisle laughing, holding their stomachs, and farting with impunity.

In front of the teens, the businessman peeled the top off his sake and, glaring from one scene to the next, turned it up and drank deeply. Setting the empty glass at his feet, he dug in his pocket for the other.

"Where did you get this?" Mohawk-boy pulled at the leather jacket his friend was wearing. It was entirely covered with pointed silver studs.

"I did it last night, thought it looked kind of tough." Tattoo-boy held up his arms and twirled like a ballerina. He ended his spin by stomping his DKNY motorcycle boots on the train floor, adopting his favorite bodybuilding pose, and growling. The two *tanuki* clutched each other briefly, while a group of high school girls who were still wearing their sailor uniforms at this hour of night gasped. Tattoo-boy ignored the raccoon dogs and turned to face the girls. He grabbed his crotch, flipped them the bird, and stuck out his barbell-studded tongue. The girls giggled and whispered excitedly.

"I think that one with the ponytail digs you," Mohawk-boy said.

"Yeah?" Tattoo-boy burped loudly and smiled her way, winked. "You think I should get her number?"

"Oh sure, she'd go out with you. You're just the boy daddy would want to meet." They both laughed loudly.

The conductor announced the next stop and the train slowed. Emptying his new sake the businessman squeezed it hard. The Haunted Parasol never took his one gawking eye off him. The two poser punks were still laughing over their joke.

The businessman stood on unsteady feet and tried to cross the aisle to the door. He made it only a few steps before a combination of drink and the switching of tracks threw him into

Tattoo-boy. The man bounced off the homemade studded jacket and sprawled across the floor, sending his briefcase and newspaper skidding into the circle of *kappa*. He kept a tight-fisted grip on the empty glass.

"Dude," Tattoo-boy said, as he raced over and offered his hand.

In spite of what it looks like, humiliation is never a single event. The disheveled businessman glowered at the boy's hand choosing instead to trust his own wobbly legs. He danced for a long moment like a marionette on too-few strings before locating a pole to steady himself. All at once, the entire car erupted into peals of laughter. It might have been the foolish jig that provoked the *kappa* into fits of sniggering. Or the way the man's barcode comb-over now hung long down one side of his face that caused the Haunted Parasol to shake and crack yet another of its thin paper-covered bamboo ribs. No doubt it was the stench of the man's urine-soaked pants that compelled the *tanuki* to turn up their whiskered noses and howl. Any single indignity might have been borne but all of them together were too much.

The boys, for their part, continued laughing at the thought of meeting some poor girl's father and the tears that flowed from their eyes were genuinely ignorant of the businessman's shame; even though Tattoo-boy was closest with his hand still outstretched, an enormous grin on his face.

The businessman tested the strength of the glass in his hand and then lifted it high overhead releasing a dreadful scream from his throat as he swung the weapon. Mohawk-boy dropped to the floor, following his friend. He cradled Tattoo boy's broken head, the head with the crack that was all black detail and red where the blood ran, 3-D. Not real at all. For what seemed like forever Mohawk-boy rocked the unmoving teen and stroked his wet cheek with his thumb. Everyone watched as the tears in his eyes continued to fall despite changing intent halfway down.

the bean washer

The old man shuddered himself awake. *This is how it's gonna be from now until April,* he thought. With his good leg he kicked off the torn and sour-scented blanket and located his cap, tangled in the web of his coat pocket. He pushed himself up. Several minutes he spent examining the sky and toeing the frost covered rocks.

"Today is going to be a Long Day," he said and pulled the cap low on his forehead.

The old man's name was Uma, horse. Maybe it was something else; he found his memory a tad soupy recently. Not long ago he was forced to invent and implement a series of Mind Stretching exercises. He performed them on what he called the Long Days.

On Long Days, when time was unfair, Uma would settle into his lopsided, often damp recliner—the one he spent three days dragging from the woods to prop up against the solid cement leg of the bridge—and there he would close his eyes and pass hours reliving some childhood memory. There were only a few left. But if he examined them hard enough, pushed forward and back like kicking himself higher on a swing, he sometimes remembered something that had been lost. Just last week he recalled picking baskets full of the rubbery stemmed, rancid smelling *dokudami-*lizard tail plant as a young boy. He was on the brink of revealing the smile that awaited the treasure, when the 5:00 PM train whistle blew, and he had to make his greetings.

Yes, occasionally scraps of memory were restored, but never the important stuff and never his name. It was always Uma.

Horse. Cruel how invariably during a Mind Stretching session he'd stumble across a mirror. A face like a serving plate, much too large; and a chin like one of those fancy Western doorknobs. No one had ever met a Japanese boy with a nose like that.

Uma grabbed his knotted stick—the one he spotted washed up on his side of the Abe River three years ago—and hobbled over to his favorite Peeing Bush to begin his day.

The sky was low and a darker shade of slate than even the wettest river rock at his feet. "Yep, today is going to be a Long Day. Today is going to be a day for remembering."

This had become mantra-like during the last fifteen years. But today was the first time that Uma was right.

"Ahoy, matey!"

"What the—," Uma started, zipped up his trousers. "Do you know what time it is?"

Adzuki Arai held up his boney wrist to his ear and shrugged. "No idea."

"And when did you start talking like a pirate?"

Adzuki laughed and shook his woven bamboo basket, filled with red beans. It was only recently that Uma began seeing the tiny man-creature in the daylight. He found him even uglier than at night when shadows were kinder. Aside from his potato-like head, he had eyes that bugged out like one of the telescope-eyed goldfish they sold at summer festivals. Worse, the whites were a constant muddy jaundice-color. And then there was his hideous little body, all gristle and corners. But you had to admire the little guy's nerve. No matter what the weather he always wore the same rectangle of rough linen folded in half—a hole for his monstrous head—tied in the middle with a cord, thus concealing all but his scrawny arms and legs. He never wore shoes.

"I got you a present," Adzuki Arai said.

"Well, if wonders never cease." Uma was feeding twists of old newspaper into the campfire and stabbing them into place with his walking stick.

"Huh?"

"There may not be much left in my ol' noggin, but I do

remember hearing stories about you, hanging out by the river, up all night washing those"—Uma knew better than insult his friend's hobby—"beans."

Adzuki, assuming he was being praised, smiled wide, two crooked rows of muck-colored teeth stretched from ear to dreggy ear. *How could you not love him?*

"And what was that song you used to sing?" Uma poured hot water from the kettle over yesterday's tea leaves.

"Oh, yeah, 'Shall I wash the beans, or shall I eat the human beings'?" Uma filled two small teacups and handed one to his friend.

"What can I say? I'm a poet." Adzuki carefully dipped a bean into his tea and polished it with his thumb.

"First you come wandering around here in the bright of day and next you go and get me a gift? What happened to the guy of legend? The creepy guy?"

"That was the old me," Adzuki said. "I'm a new man."

Uma coughed. "So, um, where's this present you're so excited about?"

The little man whistled and from the tree line came bounding a gigantic, filthy, not-quite-white dog.

"You're kidding me," Uma said.

"He's adorable, don't you think?" Adzuki set his tea and basket of beans on the low makeshift table—a large sheet of plywood precariously balanced on several uprighted stones. He braced himself for the impact. "I call him Mame." The little man was twisting and giggling under the creature's enormous paws and enthusiastic ear licks.

"He's dirty," Uma said. "And he smells like . . . dead things."

"That? Yeah." Adzuki managed to escape the canine and returned to his tea. "I found him in the woods, rolling around in Masuda-san. All he needs is a good bath and a little affection."

"Masuda-san?!" Uma spilled hot tea all down his good leg.

"He's that fishing guy with the ponytail, right?"

He is, Uma thought. *He was?* Masuda lived an entire bridge over, a good forty-minute walk. While Uma never liked to make the trip, he remembered how the eccentric man with his greasy, tied-back hair would visit occasionally, anytime his son brought by too many boxes of sticky rice cakes. *These things don't keep, you know?* Uma would provide cup after cup of ever-weakening tea and the two would eat and drink and make awkward yet cheerful conversation.

"What do you mean?" Uma asked.

"I'll give him a bath," Adzuki said. "Fix him right up." He scratched behind one large floppy ear.

"No, about Masuda," Uma said. The 6:47 would be leaving the station very soon now. Uma didn't have much time. "Who did it?"

"Probably teenagers. They're bored these days, too many video games. Need a new thrill, I suppose."

A train whistle sounded. Uma stood, adjusting his cap and straightening his clothes. He needed *not* to think about that right now. "Do I look okay?"

"Lovely," Adzuki said, more interested in his new pet than his old friend.

Taking up his walking stick, Uma left the camp and positioned himself atop his Greeting Rock. Large and flat, it provided firm footing and was just far enough off to the side of the bridge as to make him easily noticeable. If anyone decided to glance down from above, they'd see a cheerful old man waving and bowing as the train flew by. If one of those people happened to be his wife then she would be most relieved to discover her thinner, older, mostly amnesic husband and take him home, because Uma couldn't even remember exactly where home was. Although he was sure he was married.

Part of the Mind Stretching routine was to uncover this as well. He suspected some kind of accident, some kind of blow to the head. A fall maybe, it would explain the leg, too. But he was fairly sure he had a wife and a house and there might be a child. Years ago when he tried to get help from the police box at the train station they sat him down and began making phone calls. Uma knew what happened in hospitals. He panicked, knocked over an officer and fled. Even if he wanted to he couldn't go back there. No, there was only one of two ways he was going to be rescued. Either he would remember or someone he knew would recognize him and take him home.

It just made sense that morning and evening rush hours were his best chances. Him being lost and all, his wife would need to work. There's no way she could afford to live in the city, and so like everyone else she would commute, right here, right over his head.

Uma bowed and waved at the 7:05 and then at the 7:15. He was still rattled by the news of Masuda and so he continued his silly display of waves and salutes, bows and curtsies until nearly nine o'clock. By then the interval between trains had lengthened and the passengers grew sparse. Adzuki yelled over that he was taking Mame for a walk and a bath and that he'd be back for dinner. The old man allowed the two to scamper over the rocks and into the forest that lined one side of the river before he returned to camp.

≈

The tragedy of Masuda-san notwithstanding, Uma had what he mistakenly believed to be one of the best days of his recent life. After a hurried breakfast of miso-flavored instant ramen, he managed four hours of rapt concentration in the recliner. Bundled in his driest blanket, the cap now covering his eyes, he stretched and investigated the weed-picking memory until by 2:30 he was able to recover the foyer of his childhood house, its packed clay floor, a blue ceramic umbrella stand, and a row of neatly arranged shoes. There was even a strong smoky aroma of incense in the air. Cypress.

The idea of real progress sent him into an entirely better mood—made him think thoughts like, *maybe the dog wouldn't be so bad, once it was cleaned up and all. It would certainly be a nice gift for his son, or daughter, or perhaps just his wife if there really weren't any children.*

Events seemed to be culminating in a very quick and decisive way. Today his luck would tip. He was sure of it. A new pet, the crack in his forgetfulness, even Adzuki Arai turning over a new leaf; tonight they would celebrate.

And so Uma set out to gather more firewood and pay a visit to the Chinese restaurant that had been kind to him in the past. On the way back, a bundle of branches under one arm and a small bag of day-old pork buns dangling from his wrist, Uma came across a fisherman. The fisherman, too, was swept up in the old man's high spirits and asked if he could contribute his part to the evening's festivities. While he couldn't attend, he presented Uma with three freshly caught trout, each the length of the old man's forearm, shiny and speckled brown. If it wasn't for his bum leg Uma would have skipped back to camp that day.

There were still two hours before the 5:00 PM train left Shizuoka station and no sign of Adzuki or the dog. Uma dug out all his best plates and saucers. They didn't match but they weren't chipped either. He positioned two long, softly curving candles he kept for special occasions on either side of the pork buns. The pork buns he stacked into an attractive pyramid on his favorite lacquer serving tray. Tiny packages of instant miso soup were squeezed into bowls awaiting only a good slosh and stir of hot water. The trout were cleaned and salted and laid in a bed of tinfoil curled all along the edges. He even changed the tea leaves in the kettle.

Uma hummed a song whose name escaped him as he straightened and arranged the table once more, then with a glance at the sun hurried to the Greeting Rock to finish up his evening's work. He couldn't shake the feeling that something was going to happen.

Tonight Uma was in rare form. Aside from his normal performance of bowing and waving, he suddenly whipped off his cap and juggled it along with two pieces of invisible something. At one point, when his gut told him for sure that his wife was on the approaching train, he covered the end of his walking stick with the cap and tried to balance it straight up on his chin. He had never been so hopeful. Uma had no way of knowing that this would be the last time he'd ever greet trains again.

So it was at 7:46, rising from a particularly deep bow that the old man noticed Adzuki returning to the campsite. His ever-present bamboo basket in hand, he chatted earnestly to a whiter and fluffier version of this morning's dog.

It happened so fast that Uma was unable to even step off the

Greeting Rock and attempt to reach camp. After briefly admiring the carefully laid out array, Adzuki Arai was busying himself with the fire. His back was turned to the animal. Oblivious.

Uma, though, witnessed the beast sniff its way around the top of the table, knocking over both candles and a bowl of soon-to-have-been miso soup before finding and devouring the fancy pile of pork buns. Uma swayed. He croaked "No," but he was too far away to be heard. Immediately the animal discovered the trout fillets on the far side. To reach them, however, he had to heave both paws onto the edge of the table, thus disrupting the wobbly workmanship and causing the entire flat of plywood to tilt sharply, sending the canine's next course hurdling in a high arc over its head and into the dirt. Everything else slid quickly to the ground in a noisy and messy line. The beast wasted no time in pouncing over to the fish and consuming them—pebbles, sand, tinfoil and all.

"Stop!" The adrenalin hit Uma in an instant. "STOP!"

Adzuki Arai looked up. The dog continued its work on the fish.

And at that moment it all came back to him. A nostalgic slip somewhere inside his brain pumped a caustic, maddening fluid-heat throughout his body. All at once it dissolved his vision with a spilling of calligraphy ink and shot strength into his puny old-man muscles. It was familiar and it was comfortable.

Sixty-eight years hammered in his chest and froze his trembling hands as he marched his way screaming and stabbing the rocky ground with his stick. *I will show that stupid beast who's boss!*

His childhood was spent in the wrong place with the wrong face and a father with an explosive temper, a mother who cowered, and far too many siblings who were all much better at escape and blame than he was. Early on came a learned resolve, often whispered and underlined in words from his grandmother, that he would never be lucky, that he would never succeed.

Escape came way too early with the rip of whiskey down his throat, his two-faced friend. A meal too bland or a bath drawn too warm were simply triggers, reasons. The cycle as addictive as the substance—shattering, splintering, bruising. Exhaustion. Guilt, remorse, and the niggling self-hate that thickened and glued itself to every scrap of hope he once had. It suffocated any chance, any change; it needed urgently someone else to blame.

Even the moment that finally ended the loop was revealed. It was simply a small picture, black with a white frame, thrown in his face. And she left. Uma examined the picture for hours afterwards trying to discover where the series of sketchy white lines had gone. They had been there for the past three months. They promised that everything would be all right. He really believed that everything would be all right.

The old man began to cry. But still he could not stop. Battling tunnel vision he found the animal.

"You!" he screamed, pausing three steps from the beast. Uma was a giant, his heart pummeling the inside of his chest. He raised the walking stick overhead.

The dog, for the record, was not new to this kind of treatment. Years of abuse had honed its sense of danger to a very high degree. So high, in fact, that when the animal noticed the walking stick clenched in the old man's bloodless, two-fisted grip, and saw it slicing fast at its back—such a predictable angle— it was still able to gobble up the last of its pilfered meal before ducking sideways and allowing the weapon to crack and splinter on the rocks under foot. The dog gave an exaggerated yelp. And knowing, too, that in such situations it was always best to take leave when the chance arose, it fled quickly across the dry river- bed and back into the forest.

"What are you doing?" Adzuki stood, the bamboo basket slid- ing off his bare knees. He didn't even glance down at his precious red beans as they scattered across the gravel and dirt.

"I . . ." Uma couldn't look the little man in the eyes. "I don't know."

"It's no wonder you don't have any family or friends," Adzuki Arai said and he too left.

Uma stood for quite a while listening to the trains clack and rumble overhead. And for once he didn't think about who was riding them or who might recognize him if he waved and bowed and appeared a jolly old man, perfectly all right, just temporarily in residence under a bridge.

He waited but there was no sign of Adzuki Arai or the dog.

The sun sank behind the silver rectangle buildings of the city and the biting cold returned. Uma spent the next hour-and-a-half picking up and counting the small red beans that littered the gravel. Occasionally he'd blow on one and rub it gently with the tail of his shirt before dropping it into the basket Adzuki had left behind. Finished, he limped his way—walking stick free—to the Thinking Chair, wrapped himself in a blanket and tried very hard to simply forget.

≈

Uma hadn't realized he was sleeping until he was woken by the sound of someone approaching. Resisting the urge to look, he kept his eyes closed and allowed his exhausted heart to panic weakly in his chest. The footsteps ground deeply into the soft part of the riverbed. They were slow. Almost as if someone were sneaking up on him. Still, he kept his eyes screwed tight, gripped two handfuls of blanket in his fists. Soon the stranger was close enough that he could hear his short-winded breath. And then the walking ceased and Uma heard the sound of something heavy being dropped to the ground.

"Ahoy." Adzuki Arai was standing there with his child's hands clamped to his scrawny hips. At his feet lay a crumpled pile of tarp, unmoving.

"Still with the pirate talk, I see," Uma said. "What's . . ." He didn't finish the question.

"Peace offering," Adzuki said giving the heap a kick. "Or another present if you like."

Just then the tiny man glanced over at the makeshift table that had been righted and saw his basket full of beans in the center.

"You didn't?" he said hurrying over to finger his treasures. When he looked up again his yellow eyes were glazed and he blinked several times. "Six hundred and seventy-three?"

"Exactly."

"Tonight we celebrate!" The odd little man leapt up and back to the bundle on the ground.

"Adzuki," Uma said. "You didn't . . ."

"I know, I know. I promised I wouldn't. So much for being a new man, huh?" With that he knelt down and peeled away part of the tarp.

Uma felt himself swoon.

"I thought it was the dog," he said, relieved.

Adzuki Arai gave him a raised eyebrow. "You really are a queer one, you know?"

"But where is he? Where's the dog?"

"He doesn't think you like him very much. He's over there." Adzuki Arai pointed back to where it had vanished several hours earlier.

"Do you think he'd come back?" Uma asked. "If I apologize?"

"Sure." Adzuki stood and whistled. The dog came bounding back into the camp.

"Thata boy," Uma said, holding the back of his hand out so that the animal could lick it. "Yeah, I'm sorry too. You must have been starving." The old man scratched the dog under the chin. "He smells much better than this morning," Uma said.

"We found some soap and stuff."

"Oh." Uma rubbed the mutt's boney sides. "So, um, who's that?" He motioned to the bundle.

"This is the fellow who did Masuda in. I caught him digging around his tent when I was looking for something to wash the pup with."

Out of habit Uma reached for his walking stick even though it was only good for poking now, and used it to move away more of the blue tarp. He gasped. Instantly, he recognized the face. It was the kind man he had run into just hours before, the one who offered him the fish for the party. Uma was now very glad it had been the dog that had eaten Masuda-san's last meal and not him. He was also grateful the thief declined his invitation to dinner.

"You know, I had a dog once," Uma said.

"Really, you never mentioned it before." Adzuki was rummaging through the utensils.

"Yeah, it just came to me. His name was Taka. Takahiro."

"That's not a very good dog name if you ask me," said Adzuki.

"We can call this one Taka if you want."

"Naw," Uma said. "That's a name better left forgotten."

Adzuki Arai returned with a large knife tucked into his belt and dragged the tarp deeper into the shadow under the bridge.

"Here, I'll get started. Why don't you get the fire stoked back up? Do you have any of that teriyaki sauce left? This one might be a little gamey."

Uma made his way to the fire and began twisting more newspaper kindling to toss in. The fluffy white mutt sat beside him so that he warmed the old man's leg nearly up to his waist. Uma smiled down at the dog, rubbed one thumb back and forth across its forehead.

"We're gonna eat good tonight, aren't we, boy?"

yaichiro's battle

Yaichiro's heel sunk into the loose rock on the narrow footpath that ran through Ikidomari Hills. He closed his eyes, clutched tight the tiny carved sculpture to his chest, and took the fall on his shoulder. The shoulder didn't break but after that it didn't hang properly either. The young man pushed himself up with one hand and continued along the dark, unfamiliar pass.

He needed a dog.

"I'm never going to make it." Yaichiro immediately regretted speaking out loud when, sure he'd heard a chuckled agreement from behind, he swung around and nearly lost his footing again. No one was there.

It was all his fault.

One month earlier, Yaichiro, his wife, and their four-year-old daughter, Michi, were celebrating the Autumn Harvest Festival. It was the year's biggest event and everyone in the village was there. At the end of a long day of dancing and drums, home-made sweetmeats, and warmed sake his wife advised him that it was time to return home and spend the rest of the evening with his family. Yaichiro would have gone, too, if his boss hadn't been so keen on watching him dance and attempt to play a broken wooden flute. One stern word and another bottle of sake and the young man was—whether he liked it or not—there for the night.

He remembered the exact moment: he was dancing in a circle

when suddenly beside him appeared a filthy old man in a tattered kimono. Yaichiro's head was dizzy from sake and song and he bumped into the elderly fellow, knocking a splintered bamboo fan from his hand. Yaichiro had half-intended to bend down and retrieve the item, but the other dancers continued their spinning and clapping in time with the drumbeat, and he was swept along.

At the time he felt only mild impertinence thinking the disheveled old goat was merely the local Poverty God. When everything he owned had already been lost, there was not much to fear from him. Yaichiro didn't give the incident a second thought until two weeks ago, when several sores appeared on Michi's face and hands and inside her mouth.

His wife questioned him relentlessly, imploring that he admit to what he had done this time. The young man hung his head and pleaded innocence, listening while she wept and listed every day of bad luck they had ever suffered and each act of irreverence on his part that had caused it.

Remember the time they dressed in their best clothes and went to pay a New Year's visit to the shrine? Yaichiro, forgetting his money purse, had tossed a small stone into the offering box and a week later their tiny shed burned down with three clay pots full of pickled plums inside. And then there was the abrupt demise of dear Grandpa. It was undoubtedly the shock of visiting his wife's ancestral altar and discovering every golden ornament, every brass candle holder, even Grandma's posthumous Buddhist name mysteriously vanished that lead to his collapse. Who carries the entire contents of a family altar to the river to clean anyway? Yaichiro kept his head bowed and apologized once more for each sin named.

The next day the local doctor was called. He brought with him the blind woman who was said to possess powers far greater than his own. Several minutes were spent examining the child until they both agreed Yaichiro's household had been visited by the God of Smallpox.

Ruined with guilt, the young man tended the girl day and night while his wife remained for hours on end at the local shrine paying proper respect to the deity in hopes that mercy would be granted. In order to expel the illness Yaichiro dressed the child in red and helped her to color small *hoso-e* pictures while reciting prayers. When she recovered, these depictions of the great warrior Minamoto no Tametomo bravely defeating the stick-thin, pox-marked god would be burned and floated down the river.

But Michi didn't get better. Instead her blisters grew and multiplied until one day the rash color turned from red to purple— a most unfortunate omen. Both the doctor and the sightless seer were called upon once more. They clucked their tongues and knitted their brows and without so much as touching the small child to see if she still held a fever, they announced with smug agreement that tonight would prove her fate, tonight would be the battle. By tomorrow morning everyone would know the outcome, would know if this frail little girl or the God of Smallpox won.

Yaichiro snapped. He would no longer pay homage to this god of death. Against all caution and common sense, Yaichiro kissed the girl on the forehead, rummaged through an old chest of drawers, and snuck out of the house. He needed a dog.

It was popular knowledge that the God of Smallpox despised dogs. This he learned when, soon after Michi was diagnosed with the disease, each canine in the village was either destroyed or chased with such vigor and hate that it did not dare return.

Yaichiro set out.

After ten hours of walking, after dozens of cuts and bruises, as well as the one shoulder that now jutted out funny on top and shot tingles down to the tips of his fingers, he crested the final hill. Overhead a nearly full moon slipped from behind the clouds lighting up the town below. He made it. As if to offer further encouragement, rising up on the wind he heard a dog howl. It was a sign, he thought. Yaichiro smiled to himself.

"I need a dog and that one will do," he said.

The *netsuke* he grasped so tightly in his not-numb hand was made from a sperm whale's tooth. It just happened to be a carving of a dog. This secret trinket was the last remaining object of any worth in Yaichiro's home. And while it belonged to his wife, he knew that she would forgive him when, after bringing a dog into the house, he would drive away the god that brought nothing but devastation, and with that bring back their daughter. Michi would win her fight. Yaichiro admired the delicate craftsmanship in the moonlight and thought giddily to himself that he could easily buy two dogs for the price of it.

Yaichiro skidded down the slope and ran towards the town that was so near now he could identify the trembling golden glow of oil lamps behind papered windows. There was no time to waste. But still halfway to his destination, he stopped.

Somewhere nearby he heard a baby crying. That's when he noticed it. Up ahead on the well-worn footpath sat a child swaddled in blankets. There was no one else in sight.

Yaichiro's first instinct was to keep running. The moon had already risen high in the sky, and he had to return home before dawn. However, he couldn't shake the niggling suspicion that this was a test, that maybe the gods had placed the baby here for him to find, to see what he'd do. He tucked the carving into his sleeve, freeing his good arm, and carefully scooped up the child. He would leave it with someone in town.

The baby ceased its crying and began to make happy gurgling noises. Yaichiro bounced it once and laughed for the first time in weeks, sure once more he had made the correct decision. He held the child close, ready to continue his journey, when something strange happened.

Before he could take another step in the direction of the town, he felt the baby clutch two handfuls of his jacket and squeeze. It seemed to be growing heavier as well. Yaichiro attempted to put the child down, but it refused and fastened itself tighter using both legs to gain extra purchase. He had heard rumors of this trickster.

Against his better judgment, Yaichiro glanced back down and met the child's stare. Panic hastened his heart. He felt immediate revulsion. The body latched tightly to his frame, limbs splayed, resembling a tick readying itself for its blood meal. While the face that peered up, a baby's face, betrayed emotion no child could ever feel. It smiled. And just like that the child's eyes sunk into shadowed sockets growing jaundiced as they did. Its plump skin thinned, cracking into a web of wrinkles folding over to form weighty cheeks held up only by that ever-present mocking sneer. Yaichiro felt his stomach turn as the biting stink of decay met his nose. This was a *konaki jiji*, the old man who cries like a child.

By now it had increased its weight to that of a full-grown man and showed no signs of letting go. Yaichiro attempted to use his good arm to pull the thing off. He tried to force his hand between himself and the creature; he even tried hitting it repeatedly on the back and head. Still it clung. He recalled the stories he'd heard.

If he could just endure the burden, then the *konaki jiji* would reward him with magical powers . . . or so the rumors went. Maybe this, too, was a test. The weight had reached that of four men and Yaichiro's knees began to buckle. The fiend cackled as if reading his thoughts. Those who could not withstand the trial were doomed to be crushed alive. It soon felt as if the entire Iki-domari Mountain was resting atop him.

Yaichiro felt one knee pop and then there was nothing he could do; he collapsed to the ground. The *netsuke* fell from his sleeve and rolled to a stop just in front of his face. The moon must still be out, he thought, because not far off he could hear the howling. He kept his eyes on the small, intricately carved dog. He needed a dog.

The *konaki jiji*'s laugh was deafening now. He was truly enjoying himself. Yaichiro was wheezing. He felt his bones slide in their joints, heard audible snaps that hurt less than they should. Until finally, his breath would not come. Just before his vision failed, he glimpsed once more the face of the monster and saw that it had morphed into Michi. Her pox had changed from purple to red—they were clearing up. She hugged his neck and asked him to play. Her smile, something he thought he'd never see again, dispelled his anger, his grief, and his guilt. From nearby came more howling—he counted at least four animals. But it didn't matter. Yaichiro's last thought, before he ran off with his little girl, was how he didn't need a dog after all, not one, or two, or four.

sand walls, paper doors

"Tallyho!" sang an unfamiliar voice, enough time to realize it was indeed unfamiliar and then CRASH, the explosion of shattering glass.

Around midnight Anne had fallen asleep to the erratic *click-click-shuffle* of mahjong tiles coming from the apartment next door. One hour later, when she bolted from her futon wide awake, it was to the sound of her window being smashed in. Anne's small tatami-matted room had only one window. Sometimes on steamy summer nights, if she accidentally fell asleep with it open, she could easily reach out and shut it without so much as sitting up. That is how close it was to where she slept.

Anne watched, terrified as a messy blond mane poked through the gaping hole. The face looked around, eyes squinted, and then ducked back out. She could hear the slurred conversation that followed.

"Yo, man, I don't think this is your apartment."

"What?"

"Dude, there's some chick in there."

"One, two, three, shit! I'm number five!" There was the sound of scuffling, falling, and running away. Anne sat trembling as a cool breeze that smelled not unlike beer washed over her face. That was the night she promised herself she would move out of the international dorm.

As it turned out, it wasn't as difficult as she thought it would be. A kind and observant professor had already noticed the dark circles under the girl's eyes, the way her grades no longer reflected the ambition she initially showed in class. After hearing her story, he introduced her to his eccentric sister who had a fifty-year-old house in her care. The place had not been lived in for quite some time and needed a lot of work, but if Anne was willing to weed the garden and wipe down the wooden floors now and again, the sister would let her rent it for no more than what she paid for the dorm.

There was no question about it. It didn't matter that the commute to and from the university would take an hour and a half, or that she'd be that far from any English speakers, any friends. In all honesty, Anne thought to herself, I'm not here to speak English and I don't really have any friends.

The girl fell in love with the house on her first visit. Two suitcases and one box of books later, and she had moved in. She spent an hour wandering from room to room overwhelmed by the silence, breathing deep the sweet gold fragrance of tatami-mats and something else—the smoky hint of camphor and sandalwood, ghosts of incense burnt long ago.

The narrow halls, low ceilings, and intricate lintels were all marbled *hinoki* wood. Anne brushed her fingertips against the walls. Each room was a different color ochre, olive, slate, but instead of being painted or wallpapered, they were covered in a thin layer of sand, the wall behind, hard as stone. *No pictures could possibly be hung*, Anne thought.

That night she slept better than she had in years. Snug in her futon she dreamt of giggling Japanese children tugging her pajama sleeves and begging her to play. When she woke she noticed her pillow had made its way to her feet.

Everything was just strange enough, just exciting enough, so that she didn't notice what was happening, at least not right away. First she had to deal with living with the lack of house furniture. There was only one low *kotatsu* table where she sat cross-legged on the floor, ate her meals, and did her studies; otherwise, there were no couches or chairs, no bookcases or wardrobes.

Her futon had to be folded into threes and stowed away in the closet. On sunny days she hung it outside and beat it with a bamboo racket. Deep baths were drawn and then topped with a wooden roll-cover when not in use. The water was kept clean because she showered before soaking in the tub. Clothes were washed in small loads daily and hung in the sun to dry. Anne soon realized that despite being in the country for a year and a half, she didn't know Japan at all.

What the girl loved most, though, was what she called in her journal the Shimmering Quiet. She wrote that sometimes while reading or studying it felt as if someone were silently observing her, a frequent sensation, near constant. She would not have been surprised to turn any corner, open any door, and find someone there. A lady kneeling with a large stretch of silk spread out over her lap sewing tiny stitches with a crooked needle or a man who might be mending the bamboo skeletons of heavy paper umbrellas. Instead of making her jumpy and nervous, the feeling made her feel less alone.

It wasn't long before she began to talk to these imaginary friends. She didn't think it strange at all, even when she started to name the one that felt most familiar.

With spring came Anne's resignation to work in the overgrown garden behind the house. She spent days pulling smelly *dokudami* vines from the gravel only to discover a trail of irregularly cut stepping stones leading to a small pond that had been so strangled under years of overgrowth that it was practically invisible. She imagined lotus flowers blooming on the surface and bright orange and white koi swimming among the roots. The girl couldn't wait to fix it up. Occasionally, Anne would suddenly stop her gardening. She found that even outside it was quite obvious that someone's eyes were studying her. This was also the first time she thought she heard voices.

The day came when the garden had been meticulously pruned and swept, all the new flowers sunk into their earthy homes. It was also the day something even more curious happened, something that opened the way for all the others.

Anne decided she'd have lunch outside. She spread a blanket over the moss-dotted dirt and was nibbling a salmon-filled rice ball, a book resting on her knee, when she got a whiff of the most awful stench. The girl investigated, not sure what she was expecting to find. Perhaps a honey truck had driven by. *But wasn't Thursday the day they cleaned the septic tanks?* Upon further investigation she found the smell was coming from under the house. After retrieving a flashlight, she knelt near the metal grate that opened to the wide space under the house. *A cat had probably climbed in there and died*, she thought. The grate was twisted, almost torn completely off.

The beam of light fell over stones and weeds but no carcass. In the far corner Anne caught two yellow-green eyes starring back at her. A cat! A cat that was sitting in what looked to be a giant nest made of sticks and coat hangers, the lids of discarded tuna cans and cigarette butts. *Do Japanese cats build nests?* she thought. Besides, it still didn't explain the odor.

"Here kitty-kitty-kitty," she called. "Here kitty-kitty."

Just then a small stone whacked her right between the eyes.

"Ow! What the?" Anne stood up and felt her forehead for damage. She could have sworn she heard laughing as she hurried back inside the house to examine her injury. "What was that about?" she said to the presence she called Mimi, the one that was usually in the living room, but tended to follow her about the house always a glance too far away.

Out of habit Anne cleaned when she was nervous. Throwing a cloth over her shoulder she dragged a light-framed stool from the kitchen and set it up under the only object that ever gathered dust in the room, the *kamidana*–god shelf that hung high in the corner.

"Kind of creepy if you ask me," she continued. Her landlord had kept the *kamidana* decorated even while the house was empty. She impressed strongly on the girl to continue to do the same, to change the water daily; keep the rice, sake and salt fresh. That is where the gods of the house reside, she was told. Whether or not Anne believed in it didn't matter much. She was getting a great deal and had made a promise. Dusting each of the porcelain pieces she set them back on the shelf. "I think I have a headache now."

≈

The day after the gardening incident, Anne was still a little unsettled, but resumed her tidying up only to discover a small, smooth stone laying on the *kamidana* next to the shallow bowl of rice.

"What's this?" she said, examining the rock. She hadn't remembered it being there the day before. She shrugged to herself, plucked it off, and tossed it outside.

The next day there were two stones stacked one on top of the other. This time she changed the water, filled the sake cups to the brim but didn't touch the rocks at all. On the third day, a third stone appeared.

By the end of the week the little rocks multiplied one by one until they formed a pyramid. When she thought they could get no higher she rested a small plum blossom on the top rock only to laugh heartily the next day when she found an entire branch cleaved from her *ume* tree and propped up near the god shelf.

All those clues. But she would never forget the first time she saw one.

Daily she woke up with a crick in her neck and her pillow at the foot of her futon. She tried changing pillows and using different, less slippery pillowcases. Nothing worked. Anne had never thought she was such a wild sleeper. This went on nightly without fail until she got an idea.

The idea was to safety pin the pillow to the thick mat. Now, however much she tossed or turned it would not budge. The girl fell asleep very proud of herself, thinking her problem solved. At first, she fell into the usual dreams, children begging her to play. Tonight they were tossing around several cloth beanbags when she heard something behind her, a grunting sound. She imagined a pig or a boar. It was one of those sounds that starts buried in a dream but quickly wakes the sleeper in a frantic way when she realizes that the noise is actually coming not from her sleep but from the room in which she is sleeping.

When Anne opened her eyes she froze. There above her knelt a real live monster. It was tiny and withered and had eyes like two of her porcelain teacups, bulging and rolled up to stare at the ceiling. Its enormous crack of a mouth kept pulling together in a concentrated knot and then stretching all the way back to

its ragged ears again. Not yet noticing she was awake, it continued its fight with her securely fastened pillow. The girl squinted
through her gray eyelashes and watched as its cheeks puffed out
red and its stringy copper-colored hair tangled and flew with
effort. For some reason, though, she wasn't afraid. Instead,
all she could think to herself was, So I'm not crazy! They are
real!

"It's pinned," she said after some time and then laughed as
the creature, realizing she was no longer asleep, leapt straight up
into the air and squealed like a baby pig. When it hit the ground,
it darted into a shadowy corner where she could hear the knock-
knock-knock of overgrown and greasy teeth or was it the imp's
horribly knobby knees banging together?

"It's okay. I won't hurt you," she said, sitting up in her futon.

Anne named him Karl because he so reminded her of her
first best friend, a red-headed boy that was also terribly shy and
suffered just as deeply from multiple cow licks.

She spent a day in the library and found out that he was a
makuragaeshi—a trickster who derives his pleasure from removing a person's pillow and placing it at their feet. She finally solved
the problem by sleeping with no less than six pillows. A joker
maybe, but Karl was kind. He'd misplace two or three but would
always leave the rest for the girl to sleep with.

On occasion, usually when she was dreaming that something
in her refrigerator had spoiled, the girl would wake to see him
curled up beside her. Karl looked frail, his ropey limbs all twisted
in slumber, his mouth agape, his gusty snores vile. She would
cover him with part of her blanket, turn over and go back to
sleep.

That is when they began to trust her.

For two years she floated through the house. She cleaned,
she studied, and she played. She wasn't lonely at all. Anne par-
took in games with the *zashiki warashi*, the ghostly children that
came to her in dreams. She fed scraps of food to the *oni* children who lived in the nest under the house and snuck inside to
cause all sorts of havoc. Sometimes it was as innocuous as piling
rocks upon the *kamidana*. Other times she'd find the toes of all
her shoes stuffed full of pickled plums, or wake to discover the

garbage can was turned over because they were looking for used tea leaves or coffee grinds to rub through their hair.

The girl wasn't surprised at all when one day, while she was cooking up some fried rice, a long *tenjo sagari* stretched down and plucked her apron strings untied. She shooed it with a dishrag and watched as it scuttled away, clicking nails across the wooden ceiling. She named him Stretch.

Mimi turned out to be an *ittan momen*. When it did appear is was simply a length of cloth that floated and flitted its way around the room. The quietest of all the creatures, it also offered the most comfort as it always seemed to be watchful of her, worried about her. Anne imagined it understood she was a foreigner. She imagined it might be a little lonely itself.

When the weather grew cold the *ittan momen* would wrap around her waist and shoulders, keeping her warm. If it happened to be summer Mimi would swoop up under Anne's long hair and keep it off her sweaty neck. She adored it.

It was the end of July when Anne got the phone call. She was repapering the *shoji* doors, a job she usually had to do twice a year due to all the curious fingers constantly poking holes through the *washi* paper. The rainy season had started which made it perfect weather. She lifted each partition off its tract and leaned it against the fence in the garden. Stirring the flour-and-water paste her landlord had taught her to cook, she gazed out the window, watching the squares of paper pop under the warm raindrops. Soon the glue would loosen and the *shoji* paper would all but melt away. Already the paste she was stirring was thickening. The phone rang.

"*Moshi moshi,*" Anne answered.

"The Emperor is coming!" It was her professor's sister, her landlord.

"Here?"

"Next year. They want to extend the bypass." The lady paused. "Yes, here!"

"They're going to extend the bypass?" You mean the one that stops down the road from me, Anne thought.

"Yep, right over the house. The city is buying up all the land and if I told you how much I was getting for it. Boy, you'd—"

"What does it mean?" Anne asked.

"You're going to have to move." And then less excited, like she understood what this would mean to the girl, "I'm sorry. They are only giving me two months to vacate the place. But I've talked to my brother and he has found you a nice quiet apartment near the school."

Anne was speechless.

"It's cheap and new," her landlord added.

The girl was crushed.

At first there was a great welling of emotion around her. She was not sure if they knew or if they were just reacting to her sadness. But they were there. All of them. Anne could not talk though. She could not bring herself to tell them what was going to happen. And as the days passed they began to tuck themselves away, one by one.

By the time she was packing to move she began to doubt if they were ever real at all. Maybe it was some sort of temporary insanity, something brought on by the atmosphere of the old place and the loneliness she was feeling. Maybe none of it had happened at all. She began looking for them. Under the house the nest was deserted, no flighty rushes from the corner of her eye, and even when she slept with only a single pillow it remained firmly in place.

Maybe, Anne thought, she was merely waking up.

≈

She had been living in the new apartment for two weeks. It had creamy wallpaper and high ceilings. There was carpet underfoot and furniture to sit on. The florescent lights were harsh blue and her rooms smelled new and like nothing at all.

While the neighbors were quiet and friendly, they were very present. She felt always that her space was violated despite the fact that she was so achingly alone.

Pinned to her wall was a calendar. There, the day after tomorrow, was a large red X drawn through the square.

The bus let her off in front of the old mom-and-pop vegetable stand that she used to frequent daily. The vegetables were all gone, the shutters pulled down. Every house on the street was empty, making the neighborhood look even older than it did when she lived there. Anne took out the key from her purse. Her landlord had not even wanted it back, said there was nothing of importance in the house anyway.

Anne didn't get the chance to use it. When she arrived at her old house she found the front door had been kicked in. All that was left was a crunchy layer of broken glass and a hole big enough for an adult to walk through.

Setting her suitcase down in the foyer, she opened it. She removed one of the many hand towels, took off her shoes and stepped up into the house. One last time Anne walked through each room. She wiped the wood banisters as she passed, reached up to get the lintels. It hurt her to see that the *kamidana* had fallen. She carefully righted the vases and ornaments and as best as she could, swept the scattered rice and salt back into their respective bowls. The water and sake had long since evaporated.

When she made her way to the living room she was saddened to see the remnants of a teenage party or two. Teenagers can smell out these places. She could easily imagine them on their cell phones calling up friends, more friends. What a find. There were beer cans scattered about the floor and cigarette holes in the tatami mats. Someone had ripped holes into every square of the *shoji*, and some of the thin frames were splintered and broken. By the footprints she could tell that whoever had done this hadn't even bothered to remove their shoes before entering the house.

Anne sat and cried for a bit. There wasn't much left. She tried to talk to her old friends, pretending they were real again. She even listened hard for the flapping sound of Mimi or the click-like walking of Stretch. Nothing.

After an hour or so, she got up and returned to the foyer. She flipped closed the soft cover of the suitcase and began to zip it up. Seeing there was a towel hanging out, she tucked it back inside. Suddenly she felt a tiny hand curl around her pinky. It squeezed slightly and let go. Anne smiled.

"Everyone on board?" she asked, but there was no answer.

The suitcase was easily twice as heavy on the way back to her apartment. She didn't mind. From the handle that pulled it along came the occasional vibration that she recognized was the playful giddiness of a dozen *oni* children. On the bus she lay the suitcase across her knees and felt its weighty warmth. She gently petted the top of the bag, identifying from the shiver or poke each of her friends inside. Anne could not wait to get home.

her favorite

Her favorite was Toshi, the youngest of four children. The sweetest by far. The others had all left one by one. Tokyo called. Tatsuya's reason was a trading company with a name written left to right and a job title she never fully understood. Jun, with the brains, was accepted at Waseda University. Mika's excuse: a really nice man. They didn't want to go, they said. But she didn't believe it, not for a minute. It wasn't such a difficult decision to make—marriage, work, school, or a mother who sacrificed most of her life and most of her health for her children. It was simply a choice, and she had not been chosen.

Toshi remained, though. And he was the only success in the entire family. He started his own TV show on a local station. Since then, the old woman could not go anywhere without being recognized—a seat on a crowded train, an extra *daikon* slipped into her bag at the vegetable stand. She was famous.

Fishing with Toshi reruns daily, the live show Sunday mornings. It was such a good program too. He had the girl that worked part-time at the bait shop as cohost. She was strikingly beautiful and liked to play dumb. The old woman laughed remembering the episode when her son asked for a *kisu*—a smelt-whiting, and the young girl leaned over and pecked him on the cheek. Oh, the stir that caused at the tea shop that day. Koike-san even asked if she should visit the bank on the way home to get some freshly pressed money to give at the wedding.

They laughed and laughed and as the day grew short and their tea steeped until only hot water poured from the pot, they talked long about Toshi's impending marriage and the mischief of his grandchildren not yet born.

The old woman stabbed at the panel of her adjustable bed, and it whirred into its upright position. Toshi had given it to her this past Respect-for-the-Aged-Day. And the TV too. It had a wide screen. She fumbled for the remote control that had been fitted with a metal ring, a long ribbon, and then looped around her neck. Toshi had placed a red dot on the button for channel six. She turned it on: the weather. She turned it off.

Suddenly she felt her stomach split in two. Her right leg spasmed hard against her chest. The left one, as always, felt fine. Unformed thoughts jangled. Habit brought the frayed edge of a blanket to her mouth and she chewed nervously. One arm slapped at her side until it found the nightstand. Her head twisted in that direction.

There on a saucer lay a stack of sweet, bean-filled rice cakes dusted in a layer of white potato starch to keep them from sticking together. She couldn't remember Toshi visiting. *When did he leave them?* Always a sensitive child, he had probably not wanted to wake her. The sting in her stomach consumed her until, from somewhere, five gnarled fingers carried a soft mochi cake to her lips. The yielding velvet skin melted between quick gums and tore. How happy that made her, the relief in her gut complete.

Over and over the old woman willed herself to eat slowly. She knew all too well the stories of the elderly choking to death on this most delicious of treats. *Toshi would feel so awfully bad if he discovered I had passed away on a gift he had given me*, she thought. A tear moved in the corner of her eye. Chew.

Chew, she repeated to herself.

Chew.

Yes, her favorite was Toshi. He wasn't like the others who showed up only occasionally and always unannounced or worse, sent strangers around. The others were forever craving forgiveness or a hint as to where her fortune was hidden. It was true, there was a treasure. A week after her husband moved on to Buddha's great paradise, she emptied his bank accounts, collected the life insurance, and sold his entire set of Tom Morris golf clubs.

Before any one of her ungrateful offspring could find her fortune, she buried it all away and claimed ignorance. But Toshi didn't need her money. And that was exactly why the next time they were alone, she would tell him to pull up all the tatami mats from the small tearoom next door. There, stacked in perfect bundles and lined in neat rows, were hundreds of thousands of yen stretching across the entire floor.

After devouring all but one of the *mochi* cakes, the old woman lifted the tiny lid on the teapot and jabbed at the swollen leaves. There was a crackle as one long fingernail pierced a fine layer of ice. With effort she raised the pot and swirled it. No weight moved inside. Her tongue rolled excitedly around her mouth, pushed between her dry lips. She shivered. Straining, she managed to bring the blanket up to her neck.

From the slant the light cut through the window, the old woman guessed it was not yet noon. Toshi would be on at 5:00. Maybe she should take a nap until then. Following the ribbon, she found the remote control and aimed it at the TV.

This way she'd know what to do when she woke up.

With her aching foot she searched for the hot water–*yutampo* only to find she must have kicked it out of bed during the night. With the sleepiness a full belly brought, she let this thought remind her of the New Year's holidays at her grandparents' house in Nagano when she was a child. Back then there was always something to keep you warm.

Inside, everyone sat on the floor around the heated *kotatsu*-table. Chopsticks poked through the steam that billowed off the clay *nabe* and withdrew pinches of dripping mushrooms, leafy *hakusai*, small squares of delicate white fish, and long grey threads of jellied devil's root. Even gazing outside made her warm. Great layers of white fleece smothered rocks and trees and ground. And this time the steam that rose was from the tiny koi pond her grandfather kept. She used to wonder why those fish didn't boil alive out there like the ones she nibbled from her small plate.

She was an only child, the only grandchild, and so entirely cute that both her grandparents boasted she was a more beautiful, more well-behaved child than their own. Grandmother insisted the little girl stay with them at night. Futons were heaved from the *oshiire* and lined upon the tatami floor. Grandmother on her right, grandfather on her left, tucked in, she'd curl her toes and rub the bottoms of her feet against the *yutampo* to absorb its warmth, its heat. Her body snug, her face so cold her nose ran.

Grandmother always fell asleep first, leaving grandfather to stroke the little girl's hair and rub her cheeks with his rough hands. And there in the dark in the sweet tatami-smelling room, he would tell her stories of old Japan. He'd whisper myths of ravenous mountain goblins that swooped down from the tippy-tops of the tallest trees to steal away unsuspecting boys and girls, or about mischievous water *kappa* that waited at the bottom of lakes and rivers to catch a child's leg, drowning him and removing his *shirikodama*.

Her favorite story, though, was the one about *Yuki Onna*. The Snow Witch. The story ended in death, like all of grandfather's tall tales, but was less frightening because it was so seamless, so attractive. He would tell of *Yuki Onna*'s dazzling beauty; hair so black it shimmered, and skin so white it could hold no shadows. How when a lost traveler came across her, he would fall immediately under her spell and smile to his death as she blew her freezing breath across his face. It always happened that at that point in the story the wind would howl through the drain pipes and her grandfather would grab her and pull her close and say, "Look! There she is. Can you hear her? Here she comes . . ."

The old woman trembled in her dream and fell deeper into the story.

It was mid-afternoon and she crouched behind the old equipment shed waiting for one of the neighborhood kids to find her. The last one found always got first pick at the afternoon snacks. And today she knew Mother had been to the *dagashiya* in town buying special treats for all the neighborhood children. She made no effort to reveal herself. Instead, she managed to open the crooked door of the shack and duck inside. There she sat and practiced her *kanji* characters on the dirt floor over and over. It was only after she heard the whistling of the wind and noticed the light dimming that she peeked outside to see a storm was creeping up. Mother had not mentioned bad weather, so she imagined it was one of those freak tempests that blows up and over in an hour or so. *Better to wait it out*, she thought.

But the wind grew more furious instead, shaking the small hut so hard that the walls shifted behind her back. The light faded to red and made beautiful the crystal flakes that flew through the cracks, eddying. She tried to scream but it was no use. It wasn't her own voice, but the angry white noise of the storm funneled and exaggerated inside her head. She placed her hands over her ears and began to hum, concentrating all her attention on the dull vibration behind her nose. The storm refused to subside, the sun finally slipped down behind the west side of the mountain, and the room fell into pitch. The temperature dropped so low that she no longer cared who won the game of hide-and-seek.

She was just about to give up when she heard a knock on the door—not a random branch clapping against it. This was a knock. When she made out the sound of the door opening she knew she had been saved. Had one of the neighbor boys found her? Her father? It was too dark to see.

The girl tried to call out but the white noise had been draining her—had drained her until she was completely empty, empty except for a lullaby humming uninterrupted. She went to move, to reach, to stand, but she was only skin now, stretched across the floor and up the walls, all gooseflesh and gristle. She could feel the guest walk across the room, across her.

And then something strange happened. The white noise suddenly stopped. She was becoming unfrozen. There were voices underwater. Her humming vibrated, invited. A scent of lavender filled her nose. Warmth. A breath. And then a sprinkling, tickling falling across all that stretched skin. A giggle.

Snow?

It was only after she felt the cool expelled air from evil lungs that she knew for sure. The old woman opened her eyes. There, hovering above her was the most beautiful face, translucent with long black hair wild as whips around her head. *Yuki Onna!*

She had been tricked! The old woman screwed her eyes shut and flailed at the apparition. With only one good arm and one good leg she kicked and screamed, she scratched with nails that curled and cracked, hit with bones that broke brittle on contact. The Snow Witch screeched as she flew away. Exhausted, panting; the old woman had won.

Again she opened her eyes, blinking away the rheumy film this time to see her son. Toshi! Another trick? This is the way the fox spirits worked, devils, shape-shifters. And again she fought. And this time she made contact.

Quiet.

After what seemed like hours of trying to calm her breath, there was a still that follows only complete exhaustion and precedes certain death.

There was no wind to make the hut shake or cry, no blizzard to fill her ears. She was alone. It was still frightfully cold but because she was so very happy she let go a little. She was pulled farther now . . . the walls of the shack had fallen away and she stretched over the ground, up the mountain, down, seamless. There she found that the places where she had been pulled the thinnest began to grow warm, barely perceptible. She let go a little more. The warming took time. It spun her around and around on each exhale. It spread like numbness when she inhaled. And in a little while she found that for the first time in so very long she was not cold at all. Her right leg felt as fine as her left. Her right arm just as relaxed as its twin.

This time when she saw Toshi, she knew it was him. There were fingers in her hair, soothing, a hand on her face, loving. She tried to speak. A voice in her ear kept promising no more pain. And she knew again that she had been saved.

≈

The doorbell was broken so they knocked once before opening it with a spare key.

"It's freezing in here!" The lady said, blowing out her foggy breath and clapping it with mittened hands.

"The heater must have run out of *toyu*." The man lifted the metal top to a small kerosene heater and pulled up the tank.

Empty. He carried it into the next room, the tea room that now reeked from so much spilled kerosene.

"Ha, ha!" The lady laughed out loud.

"What's so funny?" he called.

"You should see this. I wish I had my camera."

The man returned, replaced the tank into the floor heater and followed the gaze of his companion. There the old woman lay asleep with her bed in the upright position, a tattered blanket pulled up to her chest, her bare feet sticking out from the bottom. He noticed that one foot was a silver-ash color; the other much darker. The old woman's toothless mouth gaped. She was holding tight a remote control that pointed at the TV. The screen was a jiggle of black and white dots. The sound was turned up.

"She must have hit the power in her sleep," the lady said.

"Yeah." He pushed the pink button on the front of the heater. There were a series of clicks, a buzz, and finally the big huff of the fan kicking on.

"Looks like she survived the *mochi* again." The lady was pointing to the saucer. "How long does it take this disease to kill you anyway?" She squatted next to the heater, pulling off both mittens with her teeth and turning her hands over and over in front of the warm air.

"It doesn't kill you," he said. "That is the problem." The man went to the TV and turned it off. "Besides, it doesn't matter. It isn't like I'm going to inherit any fortune or anything. She's broke."

"I'll take that TV, if you don't mind." The lady laughed again.

"You can bet Hiro gets that back. And don't think the others won't come for their stuff either. Hell, I bet Mika takes the sheets and the bed back."

"Gross." The lady was waving a hand in front of her face. "Listen, I'm starved. Let's go get something to eat before I lose my appetite for good." The lady stood, rubbing her stomach over her thick coat. "It smells awful in here. Hey, why don't you burn some of that incense?"

"Shut up. Eat that if you're hungry." He pointed to the nightstand and then went over to the *butsudan* and lit a handful of stick incense. He retrieved a small *Kannon* statue from the altar and scratched off some of the gold leaf. "Worthless," he muttered. He couldn't count the times he'd searched the house, top to bottom. There wasn't anything.

The lady, holding her nose, walked over and picked up the last *mochi* cake. She sniffed it cautiously and then took a bite. Chewing slowly she bent down close to the old woman. "What the . . . "

"What's wrong now?" he asked.

"Nothing. I think she's singing in her sleep," the lady said in a hushed voice. She took another bite of her pilfered meal and sent a shower of fine potato starch flour over the old woman's face. She stifled a laugh and blew it off.

Just then the old woman's sleeping eyes shot open and she screamed. The younger lady shrieked, dropped the remainder of her snack, and ran to the man's side. Together they watched as the bedridden woman thrashed wildly. She swung her one good arm and kicked her one good leg until she bucked the blanket to the floor.

"Oh! This is horrid." The lady buried her nose in the crook of her elbow. "I'm so tired of this."

Soon the old woman lay still again. She trembled and wheezed as her cord-thin ribs pumped up and down for breath.

"Mom?" The man called softly walking over to the bed. "Mom, it's me, Toshi." He kneeled, reached over to touch her head when again she lashed out. Her right hand cut across his face while her left suddenly came alive and, finding the remote control, struck him hard on the side of the head. He made his way back to the lady who stood with her face buried in her sleeve.

"You're bleeding," she said but made no move to touch him.

"Go get in the car."

He waited for her to leave before getting up and going back to where his mother lay, curled up now, shuddering and sobbing into her pillow. Her nightgown was pushed up above her knees. The skin covering her wasted legs was pulled thin and glossy or swollen with blood-filled sores. The bed had been repeatedly soiled and now, with the exertion and warming room, the stench made the man retch.

Still, Toshi moved closer. He leaned down and very tentatively ran his hand over her matted hair. This time she did not fight but instead took in deep, sobbing breaths. Her eyes looked as if they focused on his. He ran his fingers down the side of her face, a face that for the last year or so had displayed two emotions at once: fear on one side, numb resignation on the other.

"I won't hurt you anymore," he said.

"Toshi, I have something to tell you."

The old woman had more to say but *Yuki Onna* was much kinder, much more vicious than she could have ever guessed. Icy filament filled the old woman's ear. The delicate voice. *Shhh.* A slender finger touched her mouth and sent it dumb and rolling again, sucking and popping. She pulled a smile that split her lip all the way to chin.

Toshi's cut burned. He wiped away the tears with his palm.

He must have gotten some kerosene on his hands. The smell was welcome, even the burn. He stood up, stepped over the heap of spoiled blankets, went to each window, and opened them one by one. The winter wind watered his eyes while behind him he heard a cry and the snapping sound of long necrotic gums chattering.

"Goodbye, Mom," he said.

Toshi, her favorite, pulled his coat tighter around his body and left the house; but not before walking behind the floor heater and, kicking it, unplugged it with his foot.

what the cat knew

"Tama!" Old Ishigami hurried about the house, her tired knees clicking above the flap-flap-shuffle of well-worn slippers. "Tama! It's your birthday, now where are you?"

It wasn't Tama's birthday. The old woman knew it. The cat suspected. Today was more accurately the anniversary of the day that Tama came to live with her; not so much a kitten as a chestnut ball of fur chewing the length of coral-colored silk that had been fashioned into a bow around its tiny neck. Ishigami never asked when the kitten was born, never even bothered doing the math to find a date closer to the feline's actual birth. Some people thought it was bad luck not to know, but in the very end it probably didn't matter at all.

The old woman stepped down from the *genkan*, one hand flat against the wall, the other balancing a bowl of shaved bonito flakes stirred into rice. Out of habit she yanked hard at the front door. For the last fifteen years it stuck halfway across the track. Ishigami had learned the exact amount of force needed for it to open without sending it flying so fast into the adjacent wall that it shattered onto the dirt floor.

"Tama!" she called again.

"Good morning!" Her neighbor, Mori-san, was leaning over the fence motioning for the old woman to join her. *She must have been fiddling in her piles of flowerpots*, Ishigami thought. Mori was an overly enthusiastic neighbor. Always the first one in the street when an ambulance passed, and the first to deliver a plate of steaming boiled vegetables when someone fell ill. She was a woman to be careful of.

≈

"Lovely day," Mori said, pointing up. It was lovely, a high blue sky cut down the middle by a long tail of white cloud. A cool breeze took the edge off the heat. "Can't find Tama?"

"Have you seen her?"

"No, not this morning anyway. Doesn't she usually stay in for breakfast?" Mori began pulling off dirty pink gloves one finger at a time.

"Yes, she does." Old Ishigami cradled the bowl in both hands. She had added a can of preserved-in-water tuna to the usual mix. Tama was especially fond of the non-oily type. "He's been acting very strange these last few days."

"You know, I'm not one for talking"—Mori folded her gloves and laid them across the fence. She looked over both shoulders and then up each of the several trees that dotted their yards— "but don't you think that cat is a little too old?"

"He's a healthy cat, that's for sure. Keeps the mice away. The critters."

"Yes, I was wondering though, how old is Tama anyway?" Mori asked.

"Keeping busy, that's what it's all about," Ishigami said while absent-mindedly picking a chunk of tuna from the bowl and placing it on her tongue.

"I remember when you got him." Mori seemed to be trying a new strategy. "It was your sister who brought him over, wasn't it?"

"Shiho. Rest her soul." Ishigami's eyes rolled upwards in hasty prayer.

"You carried that kitten around like it was a baby, even fed it from a bottle the first year." Mori laughed. "Remember when you bought the stroller and pushed him around the block? We could all hear you coming," she began to sing, "'*Nen nen korori yo, okorori yo.*'"

"Tama was just an infant then." Old Ishigami felt uneasy, like she was being teased.

"Your sister, Shiho-san, didn't she bring Tama to you a couple days after your husband was . . . passed away?"

"Taichi, rest his soul." Ishigami's eyes rose a second time.

"This *obon* will commemorate how many years he's been passed?"

The old woman took on a serious look, straightened her shoulders. "Why, it will be thirty years this August!"

"Have you ever known a cat to live that long?" Mori leaned even farther over the fence and lowered her voice when she spoke again. "You understand what I'm trying to say?"

"Yes, certainly." The old woman took a long moment trying to understand. "That maybe it's a miracle. Are you saying you think Tama should be on TV?"

"No, no. Not that. You don't think he could be a"—Mori took a deep breath— "a *nekomata*, do you?"

"Silly. You're being silly. That is fairytale talk."

"Yes, maybe it is. It's still very strange," Mori said.

"Mmm, maybe." The old woman was tired of this talking. She wanted to find her Tama. She wanted to celebrate his birthday.

"You need to be careful. I've heard stories," Mori said.

"Stories, what stories?" Ishigami had lived long enough to know that there was always something true to be found in gossip.

"You know Mean-Matsunaga downtown? He took care of a stray once. After fifteen years it made the change."

"The change?"

"He said it was evil." Mori cupped both hands over her mouth and whispered. "It worked necromancy."

"Tama would never do such a thing."

"And I hear some can shape shift," Mori added, raising her eyebrows.

"No, he loves me." Ishigami protested. "He's just healthy. It's my cooking."

"I know, I know. I'm just saying." Mori began to put her gloves back on. "It isn't natural. You had better be careful."

Ishigami went inside her house to find a large chestnut tabby sitting in the middle of the kitchen table, staring at her with unblinking amber eyes. She jumped in surprise and then laughed at herself.

"Oh, there you are, Tama. I was looking all over for you."

She tilted the bowl for him to see. "Look what I made for your special breakfast."

Ishigami shambled slowly to the table and set the feast down at the animal's feet. The cat didn't so much as sniff the air. It continued its keen gaze at the woman.

"Oh, you're going to make an old lady blush. Stop it," she said. "Look, it's your favorite." She nudged the bowl, but still the cat took no notice.

"Silly thing." Ishigami reached to scratch her pet behind the ear, when it suddenly leapt off the table, trotted across the floor and out through the paper *fusuma* doors. Turning once to glance over its shoulder, the animal gave her a look she could not interpret before it shut the sliding door with its back paw. The old woman stood with her jaw dangling as she listened to the front door open and then a second later close.

Ishigami spent the rest of the day wiping down every wooden floor, beam, and lintel in the house. When her knees grew too sore to kneel, she stood at the stove stirring a pot of flour-water glue to use for patching up the numerous holes dotting the worn *shoji*. Eventually her legs gave out so completely that her only choice was to bring every gold ornament and intricately carved wooden candleholder from her husband's altar to the kitchen table where she carefully cleaned them with an oiled cotton cloth and a dry calligraphy brush. When nightfall came her body hummed from exhaustion. The house sparkled. Absent, however, was the usual pleasant feeling she got from a good day's work and her best friend, the chestnut tabby.

Several times she stood outside and called for the cat but the only movement was the quick rustling behind Mori-san's flowered curtains. Imagining the lecture she was bound to hear the next day, Ishigami quickly retired back inside her empty house to soak her feet.

By nine the tabby had still not returned. The old woman prepared a new bowl of *neko manma*, this time adding two cans of tuna, and slipped it onto the porch, careful to hide it from her neighbor's view by scooting it behind a large geranium planter. She left the light on, whispered a prayer and without even noticing the two big amber eyes glowing from the corner of her garden, the old woman shut and locked the door. She went upstairs and tucked herself into her futon.

Once in bed she could not sleep. She imagined that Tama had made his way to the new bypass, had tried to cross the street that shot cars and trucks back and forth; or maybe he had wandered too close to that dark-windowed veterinarian's office, the one that was never open during the day. There were rumors about that place. It made her heart sick to think of it. Maybe she should go out and try to find him. A slow turn to search for her flashlight ended the idea in an explosion of pain at her back. Maybe she'd open the bedroom window instead.

Just outside was the Japanese maple she and her husband had planted when they first moved into the house. Over the years it had grown tall enough and close enough for Tama to use if he needed to get in. He was a very clever cat. Near ten o'clock she turned on the nightlight and shut her eyes.

≈

The old woman awoke gasping. Resurfacing from a nightmare, all she could remember was being shaken awake. With her skin cold and her heart thready and fast in her chest, she groped for her glasses.

"Tama?" Sitting up and slipping the thick bifocals onto her tiny nose she searched the room to find no one there. "Is that you?"

The woman studied the open window. The wind had picked up, causing the drapes to flap wildly while the maple tree outside scratched its lacey limbs against the side of the house. She heard a rustling behind her and twisted around quickly. Pain gripped again.

There was nothing there.

When she returned her gaze to the open window once more

she saw the brown tabby sitting on the windowsill, almost as though it had been there all along.

Meow.

Ishigami could tell this was its disgruntled voice.

"Tama?"

Meow. The cat stood and began to flick its tail back and forth in what the old woman had always called snake-snake. He only did that when upset. Something wasn't right. But it wasn't until she squinted her eyes in the dark room that she realized Tama had two tails. Mori-san was right.

The woman felt her heart grow as heavy as a stone. She began to sing, "*Nen nen korori yo . . .*"

Meow. A gust of wind rushed in through the window and blew the cat's fur back against its lie. Ishigami then identified the second sign of a *nekomata*. It was unmistakable. There, in the room lit only by a weak and yellowing nightlight, the woman saw the ancient cat's skin give off its own faint but very distinct glow.

She raised both hands to her mouth while the cat vaulted into the maple tree and disappeared.

"No!" She pushed off the heavy futon and struggled to her feet. Her legs cramped and screamed but still she hobbled to the window, steadying herself by gripping hard either side of the frame.

She swore there was a flash of light before the roar, before the floor heaved and let go. Falling, the last thing she saw was a tall bookshelf tilt and crash, obliterating the place she had just been sleeping.

≈

Nothing. The old woman woke up disoriented, shredded gray and random thoughts. Downy silence purred around her ear so full she thought she just might be dead. Moonlight puddled around her. A halo. There was a breeze as well. She blinked hard because she could find neither hand to wipe away the dust and tears or to fix the glasses that now sat askew on her nose. Watercolor blurs. Where was she? What had happened?

A moment of icy lucidity before she jerked her head, "Taichi!" Pain clubbed her into a spin.

She first saw him while hurrying past the harbor early one morning. A young girl then, she was coming home from the vegetable market where she had bumped into her best friend and stayed too long to talk. A ship had docked and dozens of men, skin all black and salty, were in lines heaving giant frozen tuna man-to-man and finally into waiting trucks. Taichi was the radio operator, much smaller and less dirty than the rest.

"Excuse me," he called after her.

Reluctantly, she turned and saw him holding up a white turnip that had fallen from her scarf.

A spring wedding and by fall he was called out to sea again, this time for a year. Months later, she heard about the freak storm and how several of the crew had been washed overboard. Taichi should have been inside but was on deck helping untangle the nets.

Meow.

When Ishigami opened her eyes again she could see. Someone had placed the glasses back on her nose. Lying on her side, she could clearly make out the crimson maple tree, a kind of shivering lace in front of a full moon. She was outside! Carefully moving her head, she saw rubble where Mori-san's three-story-high pink imported home had once stood.

All around her as well, dust, splintered wood, gray ceramic roof tiles in neat piles where they had slid to the ground, some shattering.

Meow.

The woman searched for the sound until she found it up in the tree. A tiny kitten, a chestnut tabby with amber eyes and a coral-colored ribbon around its neck. The old woman smiled. The cat jumped down limb by limb until it was on the ground in front of the tree only a few meters away.

"Oh, adorable," Ishigami said.

The kitten scratched its back against the smooth bark. It pounced off and then came back to circle the tree several times. Each time it grew older and larger. When at last it stopped and sat down to look at the helpless woman on the ground it had twin tails and a delicately glowing hide.

The cat then placed both forepaws onto the maple's trunk and stretched long. The woman was surprised, however, to see that when it had finished its stretch it did not fall back down as it normally would have done. Instead, the animal stood there on its hind legs wobbling for a second before finding its balance.

"Please . . ." Ishigami pleaded.

The quiet that followed the earthquake had begun to fall away, first in pebbles, then chunks—a distant dog's barking, a support beam settling, a child crying, screaming. Sirens? The cat seemed to take it all in. It reached for a torn square of cotton that was lying nearby and placed it on its head. Next it raised one paw over an ear and began to rub. Somewhere a piece of loose board knocked against something hollow making a rhythmical *whump-whump-whump* not unlike the giant *taiko* drum that accompanied all summer festivals. The wail of fire trucks in the distance were warped beautiful by the wind, a couple of dogs took turns howling. She even heard a distinct crackling nearby, like chatter or applause.

Piece by piece the chaos fell into a strange song, and the cat began to dance. At first it twisted each paw over each ear, it cocked its head from side to side, shining golden eyes looking from left to right and back again. Eventually, it added its feet. One out then back, the other out then back. It began to move across the lawn in a small circle stepping perfectly in time to the *whump-whump-whump* drumbeat that filled the air.

The old woman smiled, euphoria filling her heart. She wanted to clap her hands to the rhythm, wanted to shout out her best friend's name; she wanted to whistle with both fingers in her mouth like she used to do when she was a kid. But all she could find was the laughter, the elation. She understood.

Ishigami really didn't think the scene could get any better when suddenly, into her field of vision strode Taichi. He was young and wearing his fishing clothes. He was soaking wet. The old woman's heart soared as she watched him join the cat's circle and imitate the funny dance. *Whump-whump-whump*, twist, kick, twist, spin.

Tears filled her eyes. She coughed. The crackle had been grow-ing progressively louder, the applause almost deafening. The old woman was now aware of the red stage lights that blazed up around them. Fear lasted only an instant. She felt a little warm, not quite uncomfortable, and was just about to cry out when Tama came kicking and spinning, paws in the air twisting about his head, in her direction. He never lost his perfect timing once, even as he extended his little paw; she giggled as she saw it move up and down to the beat. The woman considered declining but surprised herself when she quite easily reached up and took it. She jumped to her feet, shredded board and heavy tile tum-bling to the ground, and followed him back into the circle where Taichi continued the dance, smiling his handsome face in her direction.

Whump-whump-whump, twist, kick, twist, spin. The old woman found the moves easy to learn, found the strange beat intoxicat-ing. At one point Taichi reached out and took her hand and the cat's paw so that the three of them formed a small circle where they spun around and around. Sirens and dogs howled while the earth adjusted its feet again.

Catching the wink of her husband the woman felt the heat rise to her cheeks and began to laugh like a schoolgirl. She relented to the increasing pull from her cat, and was thrilled that her knees no longer hurt, her back no longer ached. She had no problem keeping up with the ever-escalating run. And so it was that she allowed herself to spin faster and faster until she discovered an odd calm in the dizzy, a calm where she stood quietly with her two friends and watched the world fall away.

taro's task

"Would you like to go for a walk?" Taro asked, dropping a knee onto one of the pliant squishes of moss dotting the otherwise hard ground. His grandmother looked up with eyes rheumy-white and cocked her head. *Did she not hear*, he thought.

Just then a breeze caught the dappled light of a Japanese maple and bounced it in such a way as to make the eighty-three-year-old woman look almost young again. Taro blinked several times and was about to repeat the question.

"A walk?" she said. Grandmother didn't walk much, to the garden, to the tree, back under the long eaves of the house if it rained and no one was around to retrieve her.

"Remember the teahouse by old man Sugi's place?"

"Mmm . . ." Grandmother pursed her lips. Taro gave her a few seconds to remember.

"Tonight begins the Inari Festival," he continued. "We finished planting all the rice yesterday. I hear they have the new tea in. We could celebrate."

"Is it spring yet?" Grandmother considered the bright red tree for a long moment. She had planted the lace-leaf, weeping maple when her first son was born. It was the only one in the entire town, and in the fall when the leaves turned from cherry red to the most brilliant burgundy, she could be found daily sitting there with friends, a sticky rice cake to her lips, the latest gossip at her ear.

And then there came the day when that first-born son threat-ened to marry a simpering milky-skinned woman who dizzied at the thought of work. Grandmother inflated her chest indig-nantly and joked that it was no matter; in fact, her love welled more abundant for the tree than any offspring she was so unfor-tunate to produce. That son ended up marrying a hardier some-one else, but many suspected the old woman's feelings never changed.

"Yes, it's spring. The rice is in. Would you like to—"

"*Iiyo*, that would be nice," Grandmother said pulling a black-toothed smile at her grandson.

"You! It's going to be dark soon." Taro's sister-in-law, Sanae, was approaching, practically bent in half. On her back were strapped two naked infants side by side. Taro noticed she had yet to wash properly and was still in yesterday's rice planting clothes. Her *monpe*-workpants pushed halfway up her thighs, from knees to bare feet she was caked in dry, cracking mud. Two other chil-dren, nine and ten, a toddler tied to each of their backs as well, howled as they played an awkward game of tag, dancing and jab-bing around their tired mother.

"It's going to be dark soon enough. You had better move on," Sanae said. "I'm going to fix dinner then take the kids down to the shrine. You can get something to eat there when you get back."

"We're going for tea," Taro said.

Sanae laughed. "Yeah, well, you'd better hurry up then." She laughed all the way to the front door.

Taro moved so that his grandmother could wrap her arms around his neck. Carefully he kneeled and scooped her up under each knee. To stand he pushed himself up on his bad leg; it was shorter but stronger, still he called it the bad one. The good leg was the one that would have made him the tallest in the town. Taller even than Kato-san, the handsome man who sold oil to the housewives, pretty ladies willing to linger and chat until the very last drop of oil left the pot.

Taro expected to be knocked off-balance by the old woman's weight and was surprised when he wasn't. Her body seemed to lift by itself. She was lighter than even the youngest child in the house. He then considered how heavy the children were, pulling them in and out of the bath, off the table, out of trees. And adults. He played with the thought that a person's worth could possibly be in direct measure to their weight. The more they learn, the more skills they acquire, the heavier they become—the more they are worth. Wasn't it only the very wealthy and clever who ate enough to grow fat?

Eventually, though, age begins to dissolve strength, dull the intellect, and tunnel the bones. All collapsing to a point where a person is more trouble for the hands she borrows, the food she consumes. If that were the case, he shouldn't feel so bad about what he must do.

"Where are your father and mother and that brother of yours? Wouldn't they like to come with us?" Grandmother asked from behind him.

"They're helping to prepare for the celebration tonight," he said.

Taro had not even reached the front gate before he realized he would have to slow his pace a good bit more than usual. Today, with the little old woman clinging to his back, he was fiercely aware of the wide swing and fall his body made when walking. Something he had long grown used to, and yet for the first time since he was a child he felt the hot blush of embarrassment puff his cheeks.

As gently as he could, he carried her down the gravel road that wound through the dozens of freshly planted paddies. There, terraced and framed in narrow, banked squares of earth, hundreds and hundreds of wispy green tufts sprouted from dark water, water now spangled in gold and white as the sun slanted across it.

The town was small, a village really. For reasons no one can remember, the people here separated themselves to settle in this mountain-ringed basin. A single path connected them with the outside world, but weather was god and it took anywhere from a day and a half to three to reach the city on the other side. Most felt they hadn't the endurance or the required measure of good fortune to attempt the trip. They left the job to a handful of sturdy men who trekked it once or twice every season, bringing back sugar and paper, medicines and invariably an assortment of unbelievable tales.

Taro would sit at a distance behind the village children and listen to the stories of treacherous passes and bravery. Once a horse stumbled and its hind quarters fell into a ravine. It took three men nearly half a day to pull it up. Always, though, Taro would ask them to tell about the waterfall.

He tried but could not inflate his imagination big enough to believe in a river cascading over a mountainside, how the thunder of it never faded, how a rainbow was birthed in its spray, or how the river itself never simply ran out. The only hope to see such sights and to have such adventures, the men would add, was to grow up with thick shoulders, and sturdy backs. It helped to be smart, too. The moral being, to do that, the children all had to work hard in the fields, listen to their parents, help anywhere they could.

Yes, the town had to be self-sufficient to a very large degree. The unsaid rule was that it was only the sick and very young who were excused from planting, weeding, and harvesting the rice they would all share. Everyone must contribute something.

Last week, the fields were plowed, flooded, and plowed again. Seedlings were teased into clumps of three or four and sunk wrist-deep into long, equally spaced rows. It was strenuous work, repetitious work; knee-deep in mud that made sucking sounds when feet tried to free, backs bent over in half for twelve-hour days. Taro tried to help a good many times, but when even level ground presented hazards the results on this unstable surface were comic.

There had been whispers before, ever since his birth, but it wasn't said openly until Taro's one-time attempt last year to hold the string lines pulled across the field indicating straight rows. That was the season the rice grew in at odd angles. Koide-san spent three days scratching his head and walking up and down the dikes clicking his abacus. On the fourth day he made the announcement that they would be short approximately six sacks of rice due to the shoddy line work. As if that weren't bad enough, it was also that year that an early-season typhoon hit and destroyed most of the crop. They were short a lot more than six bags of rice. Yes, it was said aloud; Taro was indeed bad luck.

Last year, though, he found a new way to help out. With a scrap of sturdy *washi* paper he cut a mask—a half mask to be exact—covering his face only from the nose up. It was shaped like a cat with slanted eyes and whiskers painted on in *bokuju* ink. He drew it with long eyelashes and rosy cheeks—a girl cat.

He would blacken his teeth and then, after dressing in an old female work kimono his mother was tired of mending, he placed a small drum under one arm and appeared along the banks singing and dancing and breaking up the maddening monotony. And if perchance he happened to slip on some small stone or get hooked in a root and crash into the mud, even he was allowed to laugh because it was a part of the act.

Taro could feel that his grandmother had snuggled into a layer of his jacket and he suspected she might be napping. Under his breath he murmured a prayer that her dreams hold her, a compassionate thought, a selfish thought. Before long he reached the bend just before the road fell away and the gravel became finer from so many hurried feet, just before town. The festival would start soon and last for three days; everyone was busy preparing.

He could see a small group of men were boisterously stringing up paper lanterns from storefront to storefront and in zigzags across the narrow main street. Behind them followed another team, having what looked to be a delightfully difficult time lighting the lanterns. Imbibing each of them was Ishigami-san, the town widower, and since then the town drunk.

Women huddled on every corner around large pots talking lightheartedly through fragrant plumes of steam and wood smoke, their hands busy folding sweetmeats and lining them inside black lacquer trays. The children swarmed the pull cart fronted by dreamy Kojio-san and his dog. Every little head tilted up, mouths agape, watching as he molded warm liquid sugar into birds and dogs and fat-bellied *tanuki*.

"Taro-san!"

Taro turned to see who was calling him. "Ah, Mr. Ishigami."

"I see you are on errand." The ruddy-faced man's eyes swam

in an effort to focus. He motioned with his tiny sake cup to the old woman on Taro's back.

"Yes, we're going to have some tea," Taro answered quietly, not wanting to wake his grandmother.

"Would you like a little encouragement?" Mr. Ishigami whispered wetly, holding up the bottle that was in his other hand.

"No, no. I'm fine," Taro said and then, noting the way Ishigami shrugged his shoulders and poked out his lips in disapproval, he added, "Maybe later. When I get back."

"The sun has already hit the top of the large oak." The sake cup was thrust skywards to indicate the mountain range that lay just behind the town.

"Yes, I had better hurry."

"Yes, you had better," the drunk man said stumbling off, and then over his shoulder, "Good luck."

Taro's initial worry about the noise waking his grandmother quickly vanished. Mercifully, the growing celebration went quiet as he moved closer and closer to the far edge of town. Taro imagined the queer spectacle they presented: an old woman, arms and legs splayed piggy back around a crippled man, his pace a painful pendulum and slow at that. Everyone offered a message in his or her own way—heads inclined, eyes closed, some of the women wept in commiseration. When Taro caught sight of his own mother—his grandmother's own daughter—he was met with only a deep-waisted bow that he guessed she held until he was out of sight.

It was only after he was well under the shadow of the mountain that Taro realized not only was his stomach seizing in hunger and his grandmother growing steadily heavier on his tired back, but also that his straw sandals were cutting into the tops of his feet. He didn't want to slow down anymore, already it was getting dark and cold and he was no longer sure about the directions he had been given.

Keep to the right, he mouthed, remembering, *until you see the pine tree shaped like a* daruma-*doll, then follow the trail that leads left, the steepest one. It will run you right into the Flat.* He was wishing he had brought more clothes or asked for some dumplings from one of the women in the town.

You won't pass the waterfall but will hear it. That's when you'll know you are getting close, Sanae had told him. *If you really want to see it you can travel a little farther along.* Taro really wanted to see it. He wanted to come back and have the children gather at his feet while he told of how magnificent it was, about thunder and rainbows.

Suddenly, distantly, began the thump of a *taiko*-drum and the uneven shrill of a dozen wooden flutes. Taro knew without even turning around that the Inari Festival had begun. It was easy to recall the dances and chants, the laughing girls beneath the shaky lantern light. How the warmed sake thawed his head and allowed him to fit in. He smiled. For one blessed moment it was possible for Taro to take himself away from his chore. That is, until he realized his grandmother was no longer asleep.

When the old woman spoke, she did so with such clarity that it made him think that maybe she had been awake all along.

"I suppose you don't remember . . ." she began. Goose flesh iced Taro's neck and ran down his back and arms.

He gave an uneasy laugh, wondering how he was going to explain what he was doing carrying her through the mountains in the dark. Maybe he'd say he was lost, or maybe he could tell her he wanted to show her the waterfall. Yes, he could take her there first; it wasn't far from the Flat. They could see it together. They'd visit the Flat on the way down. And then back home. But the time . . . the sun was long behind the mountain and the clouds that blew across the moon were increasingly black and weighty.

"Yeah?" Taro swallowed hard.

"I saved your life once," she said.

"Huh?"

The old woman giggled like a schoolgirl. "No, I suppose you wouldn't remember."

"Remember what?"

"When you were born, silly." She ran one hand over the rough cloth of his hemp jacket. "Your mother went into labor while I was out. She sent your father to fetch Igarashi-san next door and then to come find me."

"I thought you delivered all of the babies in the town."

"Most of them. Not all." She began to move her cheek back

and forth over his shoulder. "Igarashi aspired to be a midwife. She studied under me. Competent enough."

"I didn't know . . ."

Taro came to a tree standing in the middle of the path. From what he could make out by the spotty moonlight, it had a squatty, bulbous trunk and was a pine. But did it look like a *daruma*? The road split into at least five separate paths. He decided to rest for a second.

The braided cords of his sandals had gnawed deep into the soft skin on the tops of his feet and all around his ankles. From the sticky sensation between his toes, he supposed they were bleeding and had been for some time. Collapsing sideways against the tree he managed to untie them. One hand seemed to be enough to keep his grandmother in place. The shoes, however, refused to come off. Sharply sucking air through his teeth, he tore each one free and dropped it. He used his trembling feet to position them to point to the road they had just climbed.

When Taro turned and jumped, intending to lift the old woman higher on his back, a blade of pain lacerated his hip and down his leg. Feeling suddenly exhausted, he shivered as the sweat had already begun to chill on his now stationary body.

"You must be very tired," his grandmother said, stroking the back of his neck.

Below and behind him was an expanse of black and then a knot of flickering lights, the music was almost inaudible now. He could just walk right back down there; tell them he wouldn't do it. Tell them it wasn't right. But what would Sanae say? He could hear her needling him, taunting, she'd start the children on it.

"We need to get going," the old woman said. And as if in answer to which way to proceed, the skittering clouds fled and the blue moon illuminated the road to the left of the dumpling-looking tree, the steep one.

"Yeah." He turned his back on the town and began up the path, hobbling, the gravel shards of glass under his tender feet.

"She noticed your legs right away," Grandmother continued.

"Oh," was all Taro could say.

"That father of yours didn't do much right in his life but being fast on his feet was sure a service to you," she said. "When I arrived I found your mother in the shed behind the house." His grandmother kneaded his shoulders with her tiny hands. "You were swaddled tightly in a stretch of cloth and lay unmoving on the dirt floor. Your mother had licked a piece of *washi* paper, wiped her face I suppose, it was quite wet, and placed it over your nose and mouth."

All at once Taro felt like he had been kicked in the stomach. For years he had listened to his grandmother tell stories about Day Visitors. He knew how some women's bellies grew big and then small and there was never any child to show for it all. Giving birth was difficult, it was nature, and nature was cruel, but he never thought . . . that any woman could . . . that his own mother had tried to . . .

"She was delirious, said you were cursed," Grandmother continued. "When I unwrapped you I noticed the defect right away. I knew what a difficult life you would have."

"So why? Why did you?"

"Save your life? Well, you were my first grandson for one," the old woman said. "I am not sure how long you had been like that, but it's usually a very quick method. I removed the paper from your face. I was impressed with your strength." She hit him lightly on the back, squeezed his upper arms.

Taro's throat grew tight. His eyes burned.

"Besides, I liked your face. You look a lot like my father, your grandfather. But he died before you could ever meet him."

"I look like my grandfather?"

"And act like him as well." The old woman laughed that bell-like laugh again. She continued to massage his shoulders.

Dragging his feet, Taro tried to concentrate on the road. It had grown narrow and there was barely enough light to see where he was going. He was thinking they had taken the wrong route. He was remembering the stories of trails that fell away into nothing, about strange creatures not animal or human.

"Your mother refused to have anything to do with you for quite some time. I took care of you, carried you around, bathed and fed you. Remember when you were older how I'd invent duties for us to do so you wouldn't have to go into the fields? After the New Year's holidays we'd forage the meadows for the seven grasses of spring? Do you remember them?" She waited. "Dropwort, shepherd's purse—"

"Cottonweed, chickweed—" Taro was six years old again trailing behind his then youthful grandmother identifying herbs she held in her open palm.

"Henbit, turnip, and—"

"Radish," Taro replied.

"Your favorite, if I recall correctly. You'd help me divide them and tie them into little bundles so we could sell them down at the market."

The tears were falling freely now. How could he have forgotten that? He couldn't do this. He was a fool to be talked into it. Promises of his own room, larger portions at meals, one turn earlier on bath day. He knew none of them would be kept.

"She should have done it. You should have let her do it," Taro said.

"Oh don't be silly, boy. You weren't so cursed. Not like everyone thought anyway." The old woman began to hum a lullaby that he hadn't heard since he was a small child.

It was then that Taro got the idea. If he just kept going, past the Flat, past the waterfall; if he followed the trail until he reached the other side, the town he had heard so much about, then everything would be okay. He had to be at least halfway there. But he needed to hurry. The clouds weren't friendly and the wind was picking up. He'd never make it at this pace. Sobbing, he attempted to speed up.

Just then a stone rolled from under his foot and sent him crashing to his knees. He cried out. With one hand holding up his grandmother and the heel of the other dug into the coarse gravel he struggled to his feet. Several minutes were needed while he caught his breath.

When he was breathing normally again he tried to put some weight on the good leg's knee, the one that hit first. He found it wanting to buckle. The man began to cry again, this time out loud.

"Oh, child, it can't hurt that bad," the old woman said clucking her tongue. "Such a baby. No matter how I tried, you always were a baby."

In the moment that followed Taro thought nothing. He concentrated instead on the whirr and buzz of a thousand unseen insects, the rattle of the wind in the trees. Gradually, though, he pulled out a sound underneath, the voice of an angel soothing *hush*. It took only a second longer until he wept, grateful for the roar of an unseen waterfall. With that came an overwhelming fatigue and he changed his mind.

It is only a few fifty steps from the sound to the Flat, Sanae had told him. He locked his leg straight and started up again. On his back his grandmother continued to sing, talk to herself and laugh. Taro stayed focused on the trail, on the noise growing louder and louder and on exactly how many steps he was taking.

He didn't have to count. Soon the moon came out from behind a cloud and lit the path showing that it was beginning to level out and widen as it turned sharply to the right. He stopped. In front of him was a wide oblong-shaped piece of land almost completely bare except for a dry tree trunk that lay across its middle and the dozens of leafy bushes and bramble scattered about. The Flat.

Taro's stomach twisted sickly when he realized this was the place. He worried briefly that there would be signs. His older brother kidded him about what he might find there. The thousands of bones, bodies even, strewn about in various stages of decay. Or, worse, the not quite dead. Taro squinted through the dark blue gloom, listened as best as he could. It seemed safe enough. Then he remembered this is a job usually done before the onset of winter. Here it was spring. There had been plenty of time for the gales, and birds, and animals to clean up.

Taro decided to rest for a moment on the tree trunk in the middle of the clearing.

"May I sit down for a second?" he asked.

"Yes, I'm getting a bit stiff myself," his grandmother said behind his ear. She adjusted herself on his back. "I'm going to be okay, you know?" Her voice was hoarse. Taro thought she, too, might be crying.

All he wanted now was to reach the tree. Maybe he should try to find the falls to wash his feet and face. He had to gather his strength for the climb back down. Inadvertently, he smiled to himself when he thought of removing his load, the skeletal woman who now felt like a boulder on his suffering back. He even allowed himself to play with the idea of attending the festivities below, hot sake and salty *senbei* freshly roasted and dipped into soy sauce again and again.

"It will give me time to finish the story. I think you should hear it all before . . . you know," Grandmother said. "I saved your life for another reason." She wrapped both arms around his neck loosely. She hugged him. "As a way of forgiveness, I suppose."

"Forgiveness?"

"Yes, for quite some time I believed you actually were my father, come back to me," she said.

"You mean reincarnation?"

"I'm not sure I don't still believe it. You two are so alike. He also could have done great things with his life. But like you, he didn't."

"Huh?" The air began to reek. Taro was afraid he had come across something hidden in a shadow, something not long dead. He shivered as he was suddenly very cold. He gagged.

"I don't understand," he said.

"No, you never did."

It wasn't until Taro reached the fallen trunk he wanted so badly to sit on and was turning around to set the old woman down, that he realized something was quite wrong. His grandmother refused to let go.

"Are you really so dim as to think *you* are here to dispose of *me*?"

The old woman's breath turned into a wheeze. The stench of rot, he realized, had been coming from over his shoulder, not from the ground below. His grandmother's entire body, once frail and light, now felt like one tense muscle. Her knees dug into his sides, her bony hands kneaded too deep into his shoulders. Taro whimpered at the popping sound his ribs made. He fell to his knees a second time. On all fours he didn't have to worry about holding this old woman up. She was not letting go.

"Child, the entire town is down there right now betting on which one of us makes it back," she hissed. "If there is one thing you can be happy about, it's that the odds are in your favor." A stream of putrid saliva hit and ran down his cheek. "But only by a little."

With that she cupped his chin with her hand and turned his face upwards towards her. Taro screamed and fell to his side. It was easy for the old woman to flip him so that he lay flat on his back and she straddled his chest, her face just inches from his. He whimpered. The old woman's once tidy hair had come undone and now sprang long and tangled from around her head. The cobalt moon haloed her contorted face, a mouth grown two sizes too big and filled with too many teeth, eyes that flickered deep crimson.

"Just imagine the celebration when I get back," she said.

"But why?" Taro managed to ask.

"You let me down once and paid the price. You show up again and I try to make amends." Her exhale was a long rattle in her chest. "You let me down again. And from my calculations, you owe me a life."

"But how will you return? It's dark and the roads . . ." Taro's voice clung to the back of his throat.

"I've been resting, don't you remember?" She ran her fingers through his hair, scratched away his tears with a thick thumbnail that claimed skin as well as water. Taro retched. "You left me a marker as well."

"Please," he whimpered.

"And don't forget the most important part. I'm going to have a nice meal before I set out."

Taro closed his eyes at the old woman's shrieks of laughter. It wasn't so hard to relent to the way his body spasmed and pitched about. He deserved it. He knew that.

Instead, he concentrated on the roar of blood in his ears. He allowed it to merge with the sound of the waterfall in the distance. The waterfall he'd never see. But he could, now that there was so little time left, find the strength to imagine it.

A vision under a water-colored moon: a mighty river plummets over the side of the tallest mountain; all the way down it rumbles louder and louder until the sudden and unexpected detonation of a thunder clap weakens his knees, makes him squeal. At the same time, from deep inside the column of cascading river, a sharp crackle of lightening shoots sideways, splaying fingers of golden-static light into the forest and illuminating the trees from underneath.

But it is most beautiful at the bottom, where, despite the beating of the descending falls on the vast, seemingly endless lake below, he can make out nests of colors under its surface: flame, tangerine, gold, jade, indigo, wisteria. He watches them swim together, each trying to reach the enormous churning so brutal it wants only to push them away. And then one makes it, and Taro delights as freed, it explodes in water spray and rainbows that hang in the air for a long—his last—moment.

one thousand stitches

Mother was born a twin. Back then many things were good luck, many more were bad. Her identical sister was given the name Day Visitor and never spoken of in public again. It was soon after the rumor ran, Mother was charmed.

As a small child she never cried—as if she knew her luck. A little older and she was strong enough to carry two siblings on her back. It was also Mother, on an empty stomach, who climbed the rocky foothills and brought back a bag full of mountain eel thus insuring meals for the next month. Then there was the year Diphtheria took her little brother and again she survived; there was no doubt.

She sewed her first stitch while cozy in her own mother's lap when she was only five. "Clever hands," Grandma Fumi used to say. By seven she was piecing together scraps to make her own *ojami* beanbags which she filled with smooth pebbles. Mother, even as a child, was frugal and never asked for *azuki* beans like the other girls in the neighborhood. It didn't surprise anyone when she became a seamstress and was eventually able to master even the neckline of a *habutae* kimono. Did I tell you she was beautiful as well?

But it is never good to be proud even if it's slight and to yourself, even when it's your own parents and grandparents who enjoy the feeling. All emotions must be kept small, you see. When you are too lucky, especially in adverse times, some get jealous, sometimes the gods get jealous.

It was arranged that Mother marry the local dyer, a stocky man with a strong back and land that ran all the way over Takakusa Mountain. Gossip was kind and everyone hailed it a perfect match—a husband who would dye the cloth a deep *ai*-blue and a wife who would sew it into *hanten* jackets, *happi* coats, or pleated *hakama* skirts. Mother didn't realize then that she would never sew another kimono in her lifetime. Her hands were destroyed by the age of twenty-one.

The shop was busy and she was needed for more than sewing. On winter mornings she had to break the ice that crusted over the indigo pots, remove the previous night's material, and wring it thoroughly. An hour of this and her hands stiffened and fell numb. She would pound them against the dirt floor until the circulation returned and then she would continue her work. Worse than the freezing was the cleansing bath of sulfuric acid that every piece of cloth as well as her own clever hands had to endure.

When she wept, she did so quietly because, the old saying went, if you cry out in pain you'll never make a proper dyer. So it went that Mother did her penance watching her fingers curl and stick, seeing her skin turn a delicate blue all the way up to her elbows, witnessing again and again each thickened knuckle crack.

When Mother was forty-two years old she had her first and only child. It was an embarrassment to the family. Her mother-in-law even suggested something should be done, a piece of wet paper over the mouth maybe. Let the gods decide. But Mother refused. She felt owed. And so under the weighty spin of whispers, her son, Daiji, was born. He was healthy and handsome and he grew to love the smell and work of indigo dying even more, some said, than his father. The store flourished.

It was from about that time that Mother understood how even a single person coming into or moving out of your life could influence your fortune more than any prayer or talisman or celestial sign.

She became a mother-in-law herself one day and a grandmother soon after. She became a widow but wasn't lonely. Her greatest joy was to strap her granddaughter, Ai-chan, to her back and hum lullabies while she stirred the boiling pine soot and glue mash. These days lasted forever. Or so she wished they could.

Some say the Sino-Japanese War began July 7, 1937, on the marble bridge of Lugouqiao in China. But Mother always knew it started in the fall of 1931 at Mukden when a section of railway was blown up by the Chinese or the Japanese and one year later the Red Papers arrived in the mail. Her son Daiji had been called to war.

Mother immediately bought the best piece of white cotton she could find, one hundred and forty centimeters long by thirty-three centimeters wide. Daiji hadn't inherited his father's strong back. A *haramaki* wrapped around his waist would serve two purposes then. The first was to keep his waist warm, supported. With aching fingers she embroidered a tiger with one paw on a rock, the other clawing the air, its mouth open in full roar. Tigers were believed to travel great distances and come back unharmed. In the middle she tightly fastened a five *sen* coin. Four *sen* was pronounced *shi sen* which by different characters was also the words for "dying at war." The five *sen* would see him past such a fate. Next, she carefully mapped out and drew exactly one thousand tiny scarlet cinnabar circles.

All that was left was to find one thousand women or girls to embroider one red knot inside each of her marks and say one prayer. And then with magic woven, she would have a *senninbari*, a One Thousand Stitch Belt. Its second purpose would be to keep her son alive.

Starting at the top right-hand corner she sewed the first knot-stitch herself. She said the first prayer. Laying it on the *butsudan* altar she asked for any blessing her departed husband could impart and then she slept.

Early the next morning she had her daughter-in-law sew the second stitch. She visited relatives, neighbors, old customers. She found herself in town on the corner with the other mothers and wives, stopping strangers, coaching them when necessary, begging one stitch, a little luck. If one of the girls happened to be born in the year of the tiger then she would ask her to stitch the number of knots as she was old. This was felicitous as well. Everyone admired Mother's *senninbari*, said it was the loveliest of them all. But there wasn't time and soon the mothers and wives marched down to the girls' school at the far side of town and then to the train station to get more knots. On the morning Daiji left, Mother sat baby Ai-chan in her lap and maneuvered her three-year-old hands to tie the very last stitch.

As Mother wrapped the *haramaki* around her son's waist, she told him true stories she had heard from the other women on the street. Many men returned from the war owing their lives to this piece of cloth. A Mr. Itoh said that his *senninbari* actually repelled the enemy's bullets. Old Mr. Tanaka's son came home and spoke of super human strength. Another woman said she had soaked her cloth in plum vinegar and then dried it. When there was no more food or water her son survived by chewing on the material. He was the only one in his regiment to return.

Mother watched Daiji's shoulders pull back, felt his stomach tighten. She avoided her daughter-in-law's gaze. It was she who sent him away.

And then there was no more she could do. She again took up the extra work at the shop, spent long hours at the *butsudan* and made frequent visits to the town shrine. She collected hard candy and caramels, tins of *mikan*, and socks to fill the *imonbukuro*-comfort bags she sent every other week. Those days lasted a different kind of forever.

When the postman delivered the box, her daughter-in-law was walking Ai-chan to kindergarten, and Mother was carefully dipping her little finger into a ceramic pot of hot water, making sure it had cooled enough to pour over the first-harvest tea leaves. She set the box on the family altar and lit a stick of incense. Watching it, she took small bites of her sweet *mochi* cake and finished her tea slower than she had ever done before, not enjoying it at all. She cleaned up, wiped the table down and pretended it was a soured dessert that heaved her stomach.

The *senninbari* came back folded at the very top of the box. It stank of dirt and sweat and spoil. With fingers calloused and near numb she remembered each knot. Some had frayed or come undone, many torn off completely. As she sat there examining the piece of cloth, she noted the red discoloration where the thread had bled into the white cotton. There were other darker more abundant stains that she identified as mud. Mother held the charm up to her nose to breathe in all that was left of Daiji. Suddenly her chest seized with the realization: the dark stains weren't some foreign soil, but her son's blood. With trembling hands she refolded the *senninbari* and placed it back in the box.

Mrs. Misaki's Eyes

"Don't take that one!" Mrs. Misaki came wobbling hard and fast down the produce aisle. A *daruma* doll, all round and no legs, I saw her dumpling face knitted in single-minded intent. *Now, how did she know which fish I had just slipped into my basket?*

I glanced at the slender, silver mackerel identical to every other sibling lying whole on the bed of crystal-crushed ice; ice that I could have sworn was lit blue from underneath.

Ahead of me, Mrs. Misaki continued her approach. Her granny dress, drab coffee-colored flowers and a knotty lace collar and sleeves, flapped as she walked. This was a dress that had been loved, one that could never be replaced. Now, though, it hung a little too threadbare and a little too short for what the once thin and youthful woman had most unexpectedly become. Even her feet were obese, hanging over a pair of square, wooden *geta*. The bottoms clacked loudly back and forth, echoing in the chilly air of the supermarket.

"Good morning," I said.

"*Ohayo,*" the old woman answered out of breath. She quickly latched on to my wrist to both catch her balance and stop her tremendous forward momentum. "Hang on . . . one . . . second." All I could do was watch her lean close to the well-displayed fish and suck in mouthfuls of cool air.

The few minutes it took Mrs. Misaki to regain her composure

were a tad discomfiting. One arm taken by the woman's keen grip, I nervously shifted my basket in the crook of the other arm and pretended to be debating the brilliant pink salmon fillets before me. The entire time I was unpleasantly aware of a stock boy who stole sideways glances in my direction as he rearranged the watery bags of raw oysters and adjusted an enormous tuna head that some children had poked out of position. Soon though, the boy left, throwing one last suspicious look over his shoulder. I had been saved by the fact the teen was not brave enough to talk to a foreigner and, unable to find anything else to neaten in our aisle, he gave up his job of trying to spy on this truly strange couple.

Mrs. Misaki straightened by pulling herself hand-over-hand up my arm until she reached her full height, not quite to my shoulders. She untwisted the straps of the large purse that cut a great angled slash across her bosom, and then used her balled fist to pound lightly the small of her back. From my position I could see how badly her hair was thinning. The white scalp and white roots made the big frizzy tufts of wiry, jet-black hair seem to float above her head. They began to dance madly as she remembered her mission and dug in my shopping basket, removing the offending fish.

"You must look at the eyes. The eyes!" she said.

Mrs. Misaki exchanged the fish for its twin. "Look here. Look how alive they are. Now these are eyes that have lived."

Everything Mrs. Misaki said was a little bit too loud. This might have been because she was hard of hearing; she was "aged," as she liked to say. Or it might have been because she was unofficially the town gossip, a role she did not take lightly and what's more, was very proud of.

I didn't know how old she really was, but I did know that she was the only person her age still working at the fish packing plant. And that was despite a bum knee, a bad back, and a son who still wouldn't marry. I also got the full rundown from her on the neighborhood gossip at our every meeting, although mostly I did not know who it was she was talking about. When all my faculties were bent to communication, names and faces rarely found room in my head. I mitigated my enjoyment in the ill fate of others by thinking it wasn't entirely bad to listen to gossip as long as I was incapable of spreading it. And that I couldn't do even if I wanted to.

"Secret," she began to pull on my arm with her scratchy hands until I bowed. She whispered in her big voice. "You hear about that Shinahara-san?"

"Shinahara-san?" *Who was that?* "No, I don't think so," I said.

"Divorce." She looked warily at a young housewife who had unintentionally wandered too close. The lady backed away quickly at Mrs. Misaki's grimace.

"Really?" I said, answering the old woman while smiling weakly at the housewife and cocking my head in apology.

"Yep," she went on, "Husband went and kicked her out. Spending too much money. Did you see how much makeup that woman used to wear? Trying to look so young and all." Mrs. Misaki let go of my arm, her small fists sunk into her hips so deeply they were almost out of sight. She leaned back with effort and continued louder still. "Now look at me! As aged as I am and I never did nothing as foolish as that. Do you know how long I've been working at that plant?"

"No, I don't."

I learned that answer pretty quick. Of course I knew how long she had worked at the plant. Forty years. I had on many occasions answered "Yes, I do. I do know how long you have been there," but she always replied as if I had answered No. It felt less silly to say no and hear the story again.

"Forty years!" she said. "And my bonus just keeps getting smaller and smaller."

I also knew about her bonus, how the envelope got thinner each year and how she had recently started to stir a small scene in front of her boss when he handed it to her. Each time it was different. Once she had held the envelope up to the light and proclaimed that she could see through it. Another time she opened it and told him in front of a giggling crowd, "Well, this is a new way to tell me I need to lose weight." But today Mrs. Misaki told the story on autopilot. Her eyes were darting around and one arm was buried up to its elbow in her purse. When the lady beside us had sufficiently picked over the fish and decided against all of them and no one else was near, Mrs. Misaki quickly pulled out two pieces of cardboard that had been tied together with twine and thrust it into my hands.

"Open it." She began to shuffle her feet on the floor like a child in need of a restroom.

Untying the string, I pulled the cardboard apart to find an 8 by 10 photograph of a man probably in his early forties. He was gaunt and unsmiling and looked uncomfortable posing for the camera. He was wearing a suit that was the kind of blue not dark enough to look good on anyone. I had never seen this person before; but he had Mrs. Misaki's eyes.

"Isn't he handsome? This is the most handsome picture I have of him." The old woman was almost giddy now, bouncing slightly up and down and smiling until her eyes became unseeing crescents under her *mochi*-cake cheeks. "I picked this one out myself. This one will get a wife, I'm sure."

"A wife?" I was confused.

"Yes, he finally agreed to go to the agency."

"Arranged marriage?" I didn't know they still had arranged marriages in Japan.

"Well, if you want to put it that way." Mrs. Misaki sounded a little perturbed at my ignorance. But a glance at the picture and she was smiling again. "If you have any single friends, let me know. I have plenty more pictures and his credentials, schooling, employment, hobbies and all."

Mrs. Misaki had both hands on the photo, about to take it back when Sachiko Sato suddenly swooped in from behind, making us both jump.

"What do we have here?" Sachiko was the neighborhood rich woman. Not because of her own good sense or hard work, but because she married an ugly man with four fishing boats, his own company, and a nasty temperament that only rivaled hers. I always thought she was too skinny and too interested in everyone's business. It was similar to Mrs. Misaki's gossip but with a less playful and sometimes frightening intention. Sachiko wore brightly-colored suits with large gold buttons impressed with designers' initials. Her sunglasses were Prada, her handbags Fendi;

she slipped her dainty feet into Gucci shoes. Daily she pulled her hair back into one long ponytail that refused to move from its position down the length of her back. Hairs never strayed and makeup never ran. Even the weather feared this woman.

Mrs. Misaki covered the picture and began thrusting it into her bag again. "I really must go," she said.

"Yes, it is Friday isn't it?" Sachiko looked down, smiling at the old woman.

"Friday?" I was lost.

"Yes, our Mrs. Misaki has been visiting someone in the hospital every Friday for years now. Didn't you know?" Sachiko said.

"Uh, no, I didn't know." I looked at Mrs. Misaki, but she refused to make eye contact. She began rocking like a pendulum and shuffling slowly backwards, looking at her wrist. I had never known her to wear a watch.

"Now who is it you could be visiting?" Sachiko teased.

This was not only the first time I had heard of hospital day, but also the first time I had seen Mrs. Misaki anything less than in charge of the situation. But before I could make sense of it all, the old lady's bum backed right into a small child that was standing near his mother. The child's cries or the old woman's embarrassment sent Sachiko into peals of laughter.

Mrs. Misaki took her chance and quickly wobbled to the door.

"Imagine the bride that marries into THAT family." Sachiko clucked her tongue and shook her head. *So she had seen the photo.*

I was thinking of an answer in defense of the old gossip I liked to think was my friend when Sachiko suddenly put her pretty hand into my basket. Her maroon fingernails scraped the wrong way up the side of the fish, tiny transparent scales flew. She tapped lightly below the open staring eye.

"Good choice. See, you are learning. How long have you been in Japan now?"

"About six years. I didn't pick that one out . . . ," but before I could finish, she was walking away from me, wiping her hand on a lace handkerchief.

"Sure you did, dear," she said over her shoulder. "Sure you did."

≈

I was walking home from the bus stop when I caught Mrs. Misaki outside her house, making great big noises as she stood bent over one corner of her yard. I worried that she might be suffering some kind of attack or stroke while gardening.

"Hello, is everything okay?" I called out.

"Quiet. Come here."

I headed around to the front gate and let myself in. The smooth gray stepping stones zigzagged a split path, one going to the house and the other to where Mrs. Misaki now stood, trying to uncork a giant bottle of sake that she was squeezing hard between her knees.

"Can I help you there?" I asked.

"Yes, please. Can you open this?"

The plastic cork slid out easily, and I handed the bottle back to the old woman. She checked carefully up and down the street that ran in front of her house. When she was satisfied there was no one around, she began to pour some of the silvery liquid over the ground.

"We'll do this to all four corners," she told me, hurrying off in short, beating steps to the next area.

I followed silently and watched as she emptied the entire contents in fourths, each time clapping her hands and bowing her head in prayer.

"There, that should do it."

"Do it?" I asked.

"I have discovered I have an *ikiryou*, and it is causing me some great harm. I need to be rid of it as soon as possible."

"A what?" I had never heard the word before.

"It is a spirit, of the living. It attaches to you and does the most awful things," she explained. I noticed she did look a bit tired today.

"A spirit of the living?"

"Yes, we all have spirits, souls—you believe that, right?" The old woman sat down on one of the fancy boulders that decorated her small Japanese garden and motioned for me to sit on the rock next to her. Again she glanced out to the street. "Sometimes if someone has some great negative emotion, like hate or anger or jealousy, their spirit will actually go to the object of that emotion and harm them."

"Oh," I said.

"Don't get me wrong, there are spirits of the dead as well. If they are disgruntled about something they can be pretty vicious themselves. But I can tell this one is someone alive. I can tell."

"Like ghosts?" I asked.

"Don't tell me they don't believe this in that country you come from." Before I could find an answer she began talking again. "I am always at the end of some sort of wrath. Being as aged as I am, and how much I know about what really goes on in this town."

"Yeah," I said, feeling a little relief at what I knew was coming next.

"Do you have any idea how old I really am?" she asked.

≈

I hadn't seen Sachiko in nearly two months, so I was surprised when she came over and offered to take me. Since I had never done this before, and I was aware of the tangled sensitivity and importance of tradition, I agreed. She coached me on the proper Japanese phrases as we walked past the two paper lanterns that stood on either side of the stone walk winding its way to Mrs. Misaki's house. A miniature waterfall trickled near a folding table where a dark man with a permanently sad face sat in a black suit and tie. He took our envelopes and used a small machine to cut the ends off. Under the table he fingered out the money, placed it into a box, and then scribbled something into a notebook. I had given two thousand yen and received a small package wrapped in white with a card attached to the top. Sachiko had given five thousand and had been handed a larger package, which she slid into her black leather bag that just happened to be the right size.

In the foyer I held my box awkwardly under my left arm, my right hand against the sandy wall for balance as I removed my black leather pumps. Sachiko had already stepped up into the

main house and was looking down at me as I lined up my shoes
next to the dozens of others. Row after neat row, all with toes
pointing towards the door.

"Inside the card on your box there is a small bag of salt.
Before you enter your house, you must sprinkle it all over yourself." She had taken a lint brush from her purse and was brushing the shoulders of my dark jacket. "And remember to do your
head and shoulders, too. You don't want any nasty ghosts following you home, do you?"

I walked after her through the house. All the walls had been
hung with white cloth. Even the doors to other rooms were hidden, so that we only had to follow the simple maze and the tinny
ring of a bell to find where everyone was gathered.

The room was candlelit and cold and full of quiet people
kneeling on the tatami-matted floor. An ancient air conditioner
rattled in the window, a white noise drone that made the crowded
room a little easier to enter. Everyone was taking turns shuffling
up to the giant altar and offering incense, ringing a bowl-shaped
bell and praying. The altar covered half a wall and was piled high
with baskets of fruit, sweet rice cakes, and giant fake flowers
of purple and silver that twisted up either side. Strange colored
lights spun violet shadows on the ceiling and across the photo
of the deceased.

"How embarrassing," a neighbor mumbled to herself as she
passed us to leave.

I took Sachiko's lead, offering incense and prayers, and moved
to the corner of the room where, kneeling *seiza*, we bowed low
with our hands facedown on the tatami-mat floor.

"It was so sudden," Sachiko said to an old lady dressed in all
black with a string of pearls around her neck.

"No," the old woman said, "It's been a long sickness."

"This is Mrs. Misaki's sister." Sachiko introduced us and I
bowed and told her it was nice to meet her. I wanted to use one
of the phrases Sachiko had taught me but became distracted
when I saw the state Mrs. Misaki was in.

She was leaning against her sister, weeping heavily into a handkerchief. On the other side of her on a white futon lay her son.
He had the same gaunt expression that he wore in the picture

I had seen in the supermarket only two months earlier. And in this room of people, most of whom he had probably never met, he lay in that same icky-blue suit. When I saw that he had been packed generously with dry ice, I shivered.

"I didn't know he was sick." I wasn't sure if that was the proper thing to say or not.

"You see, he had been going to the hospital for years now. And we thought he was getting better," Mrs. Misaki's sister continued, looking sideways towards Mrs. Misaki, who was now mostly on the floor and heaving violently.

"Hospital day?" I asked looking at Sachiko.

"See, you're learning something." Sachiko nodded and patted my knee, picking off a stray piece of string.

"I remember when he told us that he would go to the agency. That he wanted to get married. That he wanted children even. We thought for sure he knew he was getting better," Mrs. Misaki's sister explained.

"Or getting worse." Sachiko looked matter-of-factly at the dead man and then back to Mrs. Misaki, who didn't appear to be listening at all.

"You shouldn't say that!" I was angry and my voice loud. I felt my cheeks burn when I noticed I had invited the whole room to listen to our conversation.

"Oh, don't you see?" Sachiko patted my leg again and laughed lightly. "He's an only child. If he had gotten married there would be a daughter-in-law. There would be someone here to take care of Mrs. Misaki. He knew how much she wanted him to marry. And maybe he hoped to fulfill that dream." She paused and turned to the audience. "He was such a good son. He wanted to get married for his mother, to make her happy."

Everyone in the room smiled and nodded in agreement that yes, he was a very good son. And while it sounded compassionate enough, at least an interesting thought, Mrs. Misaki let out a piercing and distinctly inhuman wail that told me she had been hurt by the remark.

It was the few seconds after the scream that forever changed my thoughts on life and death. I could no longer stand to watch the old woman in so much pain; yet, I felt it was not the place for me to pet her or take her into my arms. Not wanting to stare at the scene anymore, I looked back to the deceased son tucked into his icy bed. Only now, to my horror, the grim man was very clearly sitting up.

No one in the room seemed to notice. They all continued their whispers or silent gawking at the wild and broken woman, oblivious. But there the son sat, shoulders curled forward, head drooped. I noted too that another son remained less alive and still stiffly prostrate on the white futon. Since childhood I have always imagined ghosts and spirits to be shimmering and see-through things that floated and flitted about, nearly unseen. But this, I saw, was wrong.

The son's sitting body was actually denser, somehow even more vivid than his prone one. I would even say that it was more concentrated than any of the living bodies currently occupying the darkened room.

And yet to everyone, even to the fellow who stood leaning over the dead man in quiet prayer, the sitting specter swaying barely inches from his nose, he was invisible. My heart stuck stubbornly in my throat while, for a long moment, all I could hear was the fuzzy white noise of the air conditioner and my own pulse in my head. *Am I mad?*

I turned to Sachiko, who was beside me in full enjoyment of the crumpled Mrs. Misaki. She was shaking her head in pity or disgust when our eyes met briefly, and it was as if she were saying, "Don't you think so, too?" I shook my own head and withdrew from the woman. It was then that I caught a movement from the corner of my eye.

Mrs. Misaki's son was now on all fours making his way across the tatami floor, making his way towards us. A wave of nausea welled up in me, and I recoiled against the wall at my back. Sachiko shot me a quick grimace at my lack of manners. She probably thought my legs had gone numb from sitting on my knees for so long. But luckily, she was too absorbed in her own entertainment to pull me back into position. So I watched the slow advance of the dead man in his awful suit.

Mrs. Misaki's sister was rubbing her sibling's shoulders and speaking soothingly into her ear.

"I'm afraid this happens sometimes," Sachiko said.

I only half listened as I was seriously planning the path I would use when I jumped to my feet and bolted from the room.

"Sometimes they lose their minds," she said softly.

Right then two things happened at once. The first was that Mrs. Misaki looked up from her sister's shoulder with momentary soberness and what also resembled defiance. She repressed a couple of sobs and her mouth moved as if she were trying to find something to say. *She knew,* I thought. *She might not see him, but she could feel him.*

The second thing that happened was that her son reached his target. He was now making his way around Sachiko and with one hand on her shoulder; he was climbing onto her back.

The room was a greedy silence—all these pale ghosts of people who called themselves friends. The only one that looked on with any care or sadness was the large photograph propped up on the altar. It was the same picture I had seen in the supermarket. The same face that now clung near Sachiko's ear also waiting to see what would happen.

"It's such a good picture," I said pointing to the photo. My voice was shaky and unsure.

Mrs. Misaki sobbed her last sob and looked at me. The entire room watched.

"Isn't he handsome?" I asked to anyone at all.

"That's the most handsome picture I have of him." Mrs. Misaki spoke for the first time.

"It must be the eyes. Now those are eyes that have lived," I said, attempting a smile at the old woman who looked to be finally coming out of a daze.

Her eyes were puffy and rubbed raw and red, her skin splotchy with wrinkles I had never noticed before. She had not washed or teased her hair and it lay thin and flat against her head. The old woman slowly straightened her back and ran both hands over her rumpled dress. She trembled as she refolded her handkerchief and then faced the room full of people.

Sachiko, I observed, had a queer look on her face, like she might be sick. Her friend was latched on with wild-eyed zeal.

"Excuse me." Mrs. Misaki began slowly. With what looked like enormous effort she smiled until the saggy wrinkles all lifted to fill her cheeks and push her eyes into those closed crescents that I recognized.

Mrs. Misaki suddenly had a tired kind of poise. "I just wanted to thank you all for coming today." She glanced at each visitor in turn, offering a nod of her head. When she reached Sachiko, who was now half bent over and massaging weakly the same shoulder the rage-colored dead man had clenched earnestly between his teeth, she knitted her brows before resting her gaze on me and finishing her speech. "It means everything in the world to me to have friends as precious and kind as you."

"We need to go," Sachiko said. "I don't feel well."

I was able to sneak in a few words with Mrs. Misaki and pat her hands before we left. Sachiko was first to the foyer, struggling to put on her shoes. The man had both arms and legs wrapped tightly around her neck and waist and seemed to be very much enjoying the ride. I found my own shoes and was putting them on, trying not to stare or get too close. Sachiko was already hurrying out the door and across the stepping stones.

"I'm going to go on ahead," she said. She had her purse open and was searching desperately for something inside.

"See you," I called, watching her run down the road, Mrs. Misaki's son laughing piggyback all the way. I checked once over both shoulders and then felt in my own purse, relieved when my fingers located the small paper bag. I glanced once more at the disappearing figures of Sachiko and her rider.

"Ain't no little package of salt going to remove that," I said and made my way home.

devils outside

It began and in a way ended with the heart-stopping crack of a single tree split in half, and then the sky broke loose, followed by—as they say—all hell.

The day started as it always did with Mother sliding the wooden rain shutters open along their splintered tracks and kicking me awake. I was the oldest at eleven and for the most part in charge of the other children. There were six of us, and we all slept together in one room. I remember how Father use to tease us before bed, saying that if he took several lengths of sharpened bamboo from the shed and pierced each of us just so, we'd look exactly like the mismatched sweet fish Grandma sunk into the mixture of sand and ash that cradled the crackling fire.

There weren't enough futons, only three, so the babies—not old enough to complain—were pushed into the crevices between mats. It was safe that way. They didn't roll around so much and we could find them easier in the morning. That is, except Shime.

Shime was the youngest at four years old. Her skin was tofu-white, and she had a head full of blue-black bouncing curls as thick around as Father's thumb. We had never seen anyone with curly hair before. We knew it meant something.

The night she was born, Grandma stayed up until dawn sewing the baby-sized sleeping mat. Despite the fact that the delivery was so effortless, Mother hadn't had time to call on us for assistance. This should have meant we all slept well that evening, but none of us did.

That was the first night the foxes slunk into the trees and shook the branches with their ladylike hands. It was also the first night the tanuki drummed their hollow bellies and yowled until the sun came up.

From birth Shime was a good-natured child. So much so that I cannot remember ever hearing her cry. No matter how sleepy or hungry or wet, she managed somehow to communicate her condition to those around her—usually me—without a lot of fuss. Shime never said a word, and yet she saved each of us in her own way.

Being born during the New Year's festivities also made Shime an auspicious baby, at least that is what Grandma said. But she didn't have to tell me. I'll never forget that time by the falls.

Jiro and Sui, ten and nine, tended to the twins, but there were not enough backs to go around. Even though I was a boy, Shime was handed to me when she was one month old. Every morning the babies were wiped down and fed and then tied with thick cloth cords to our backs where they spent most of the day.

Like I said, this is usually a job for the females in the family, but Grandma's spine was curled nearly in half and Mother worked the fields almost as hard as Father. Sui was our only sister, but she couldn't very well keep three babies on her back. The work was divided up. I didn't mind so much. Our house was a day and a half walk from the town of Tanioku, and I was hardly ever seen by boys my own age.

After chores and the fieldwork we kids would sometimes climb into the hills to pick wild herbs or catch fish. Shime must have been about six months old at the time. She had a strong neck and seemed to enjoy my excursions, so I convinced the others to follow me to a small waterfall I had discovered. It was a bit of a hike, but I figured if we brought back souvenirs I'd escape getting my fingers burned with *moxa* incense for being late. We played for a while before Jiro and Sui, with their babies in place, wandered down to where the water calmed to drop their fishing lines.

With Shime secured and squeaking behind me like an overgrown cicada, I decided to climb higher and see if I could pick some spring grasses from beside the fall. Since the time I was small, Grandma lectured me about the healing properties of weeds and flowers harvested on certain lucky days. That day just happened to precede a full moon, which for reasons that I never fully understood made for finer and more potent plants.

When I was very young Mother used to be the main herb gatherer, but something happened and she now absolutely refused to hike into the mountains that surrounded our house, even the foothills. Father and Grandfather couldn't be bothered and the younger ones didn't have an eye for grasses or flowers or mushrooms like I did. Let them carry the half-dozen slapping, smelly fish back home; I'd stuff my hip basket with fragrant and weightless herbs, sure as I always was to win the race back home.

From where I was standing, it looked like a large clump of spindly shepherd's purse growing halfway up the rocky slope. For the past few weeks all I could collect were batches of chickweed. Chickweed was always needed as Grandma was forever boiling tinctures for Father's itchy legs and tea for her own achy stomach. But I also knew that if there was one sure way to merit an extra helping at supper time, it was to present Grandma with something tasty and different that she could stir into the evening's miso soup.

For nearly thirty minutes I scaled the rocks and pebbly soil, filling my hip basket with dirty-rooted plants, when I spotted the unmistakable purple-brown cone of a fresh bamboo shoot. My heart leapt. I could almost taste the tender, slightly bitter flesh between my teeth. And I knew if there was one, there had to be more.

I must have been concerning myself with how I was going to remove the fragile shoot with no shovel or spade because before I knew it my foot settled onto a stone that gave way with my weight. It all happened in an instant. I felt my leg slice through the air as my hands scrambled and tore at the dirt, rock, and weeds trying to find something to hold on to. The roar of the waterfall was almost deafening in my ears, but even then I distinctly heard two things.

The first was the devious rock that betrayed my foot as it clacked its way down the side of the mountain and landed with a great splash into the pool below. The second was Shime over my shoulder making a comforting cooing sound, almost as if she were invoking something or someone. Before I could plummet to the earth, I was seized under each arm, scooped up, and placed on a more secure piece of ground. Jiro and Sui, busy chasing down a dropped fish, didn't witness the miracle, but soon afterwards when I related the event, they didn't disbelieve my story. They knew.

At the very beginning we enjoyed exchanging our tales of luck and chance and heavenly intervention. But that changed right after Shime's first birthday when Grandma figured out what was going on.

Grandpa wasn't a proud man, yet he was quick to flaunt his most prized possession—a pair of false teeth. Carved of the finest boxwood and meticulously fitted over a period of three weeks, Grandpa regularly announced that his teeth were worth more than the house and everything and everyone inside it.

He procured his treasure after a long night of playing mahjong at the Buddhist temple on the other side of Kiri Naki Mountain. It was Grandma though who took credit for his success, saying it was the amulet she tucked into his waist sash that swayed the outcome that evening. With a smug look on her face she reminded us all that Grandpa's stars had never been that remarkable on their own.

Still, Grandpa loved to repeat the story about how he not only beat every single monk living in the temple complex, but also a craftsman who was once a specialist in carving small Buddha statues for family altars. The man was traveling on a pilgrimage, stopping for what he thought would be a short stay.

By the third game and the second bottle of sake the traveler began boasting about the night the Buddha descended into one of his dreams. The story went that after the god expressed his appreciation for the craftsman's hard work and dedication, he went on to assert that his incense-fragrant and flower-laden paradise was wide open for a man with great skill who worked selflessly to help the frail elderly grow strong again by providing them the means to chew a good hard chunk of pickled radish now and again. And so the craftsman changed professions.

Jiro, Sui, and I finished our meal of rice and mountain eel and were sitting around the low *kotatsu* table with our feet pressed against the wooden slats underneath, trying to absorb the heat from the popping pieces of burning charcoal. Mother and Grandma cleared the table and were preparing *osechi* in the kitchen while Grandpa and Father sat cross-legged at the hibachi, poking its embers with the metal chopsticks and smoking deep draws on their long, tiny-bowled *kiseru* pipes. The little ones wandered over the tatami mat immune to the biting cold. Grandpa had already drunk enough heated sake to turn his face and neck red as a boiled octopus and Father was quickly catching up.

It was New Year's Eve and we were all excited. The heavy cleaning finished the day before, and the cooking done into the wee hours of the night was being tucked away in lacquered boxes, ready for us to eat early the next morning.

We all knew it was coming. There was something else about Grandpa filled with too much alcohol and his cherished false teeth. He had the disturbing habit of removing them at a moment's notice. Most of the time he'd merely turn them about in his hands, coaxing out stray strands of squid or checking for chips and cracks in the wood; but also, he liked to show them off to anyone who happened to be around at the time, hoping—I suppose—to be asked once more the story of how he acquired them. He especially liked to point out the gold leaf that coated the bottoms.

"That kills germs," he'd say. "Keeps my breath fresh."

Grandpa had anything but fresh breath, but excepting Sui and the adults in the household, we all loved the morbidity of the ritual and at times even encouraged it.

"A man with gold in his mouth!" he'd say. "A man who can taste the cold, auspicious slick of gold every single day, now that is one lucky man!"

On this particular night Grandpa began a tradition that continued right up until the day he discovered a tiny hole in one of the molars and upon investigation released a family of some sort of squirmy bug living in six of the thirty-two teeth. One high-pitched scream later, he tossed both upper and lower plates into the fire and began a life of eating watery porridge and soft-cooked pumpkin, never again to commit the sin of pride.

But that New Year's Eve, Grandpa crawled over to our table and snuck his feet in next to ours while reaching over to touch one of Shime's curls—this later became a good luck gesture we all took part in from time to time.

"Ahh, a New Year is almost here," he said. "I suppose you kids want a little *otoshi dama* from your old Grandpa, huh?"

"Oh, Grandpa, it's okay, we don't need any money." Sui was never the one to cut a good deal.

"I'm sure your Father has a coin or two to give you tomorrow. But your Grandma and I, all we have is the roof and walls and whatever decides to come up in the fields outside." He sighed and shook his head, smiling.

"You know what?" Grandpa stroked his chin in mock thought. "I think I can give a little something to you big kids. Something you might appreciate." With that he opened his mouth wide and popped out his false teeth. "Since it's not exactly an *otoshi dama* I'll give it to you early."

Sui buried her face into the crook of her arm refusing to look. Jiro and I leaned closer, instinctively knowing something marvelous was about to happen. After a brief appraisal, Grandpa flipped the wooden teeth over and using his thumbnail scraped off a tiny fleck of gold leaf.

"Here, this is for you, Ichiro," Grandpa said.

I held out my hand and watched the flake drop and curl onto my calloused palm.

"Thank you, Grandpa, thank you so much." I cupped my other hand over the first and brought it in towards my chest to keep Jiro, who was entirely too enthusiastic, from blowing it away.

"And Jiro." Grandpa held out another thumbnail full of gold leaf while clucking his tongue with delight in his newly emptied and disturbingly hollow-sounding mouth.

"*Arigatou!*"

"And Sui." Despite her disgust, Sui moved nearer and thrust out her open hand.

"Wait a minute, she got a bigger piece," Jiro whined.

"No, no, they're all exactly the same," Grandpa said. "Here, let's see."

We all opened our hands to compare our flakes when Jiro suddenly jostled me. After I recovered my balance, I noticed my tiny slice had vanished.

"You!" I tackled my younger brother with the full intent of either ending his short, meager life, or stealing his piece of gold. Jiro fought back hard.

Very soon the table was upended, Grandpa and the other children huddled in the far corners of the room, and Father was boxing my ears.

The tragedy that night wasn't that my piece of gold flake had been lost—Grandpa would replace it soon enough with a new sliver—but that somehow in the scuffle, Grandpa's upper plate had been thrown and no one could find it. We scoured the room, shook the *kotatsu* blanket and even raked the ashes in the fire. It had completely vanished.

Grandpa spent the rest of the evening sulking near the hibachi, rubbing his hands and smoking his pipe as sad as I had ever seen him. He fretted out loud over all the New Year's delicacies he wouldn't be able to eat, and at one point I thought I heard a sob.

Hours of searching ended with several more swats to the head and Grandma eventually sitting in front of the family altar, lighting candles and incense and rubbing prayer beads between her boney fingers.

"It's the strangest thing," Father mumbled, emptying the spent tobacco from his pipe with a *whack-whack-whack* as we children were marched off to bed.

It wasn't until the next day, right before we sat down to enjoy our New Year's feast, that Shime came toddling over to a nearly despondent Grandpa and, steadying herself on his shoulder, presented him with his slightly drooled over upper plate.

"Where did she find it?" Sui asked.

"But I searched her," Mother said holding one hand to her mouth. "I searched all the babies . . . three times."

"It's like she's magic," I said.

"Hush, child." Grandma pinched and twisted the thin skin on the back of my arm. "Never speak of such things!" she hissed. Jiro made an effort to defend me only to be silenced by Grandma's beady stare, which she cast on each member of the family before kneeling once again in front of the altar, this time in gratitude. There she sat in curls of sandalwood smoke and mumbled prayer for the rest of the day refusing all the food offered her.

The matter was never discussed again. We all knew now to keep quiet about our experiences, our meager fortunes, and our good luck baby.

That is, until the day of the storm, when by the end of the night more than one of us could be heard begging whatever god or gracious spirit watched out for Shime to return and save our lives.

It was surprising how the gnarly ball of Mother's foot always found the same spot just under my right shoulder blade.

"Ow!" It was a chilly, dark day and I wasn't ready to shake off my dream reliving yesterday's pilfered licks of sugared adzuki bean paste from Grandma's flat wooden *shamoji*. The best part of any holiday was indulging in the sticky rice balls that we ate until our stomachs grew achy and taut.

It was *setsubun*—the end of winter and the day when our entire family ceremoniously banished the evil spirits still clinging from last year and invited more benevolent forces to reside in our home. It was the same every year, after sundown there would be a knock on the door—a pounding really—Mother would provide us children with bowls of heated soybeans and then bravely open the door. Two devils, Father and Grandpa behind masks of colored clay and straw, appeared growling and swinging their wooden clubs. The little ones would scream and cry while it was up to us older ones to throw the hot beans at the *oni* and demand they leave.

"*Oni wa soto*! Devils outside!" we'd yell and pelt them mercilessly with our roasted ammunition. The two would howl and dance around in time, relenting to our assault. Digging deep into their bags they'd pull out candies and other sweetmeats and toss them back chanting "*Fuku wa uchi*! Good luck inside!" before disappearing into the night only to return later, much redder, utterly happy and ready to share in the goodies.

We were all deathly afraid of *oni*—at least we were of the real ones. We had watched as Grandpa cast the devil tile, the *oni gawara*, he placed on the roof to frighten the devils away. It gave us nightmares for a week. But Grandma was the real provoker of our imaginations.

If a persimmon disappeared from the family altar or a hole found its way into the feathery paper of a *shoji* door, she would sit all of us down and explain what happened to children who disobeyed. With eyes closed—as if remembering—she would describe what hid in the mountains, crouched in the caves, what it was exactly that had eaten our dog two years before.

The oni *come in two kinds. But first let me tell you how they are the same: there is no difference in size; they are all as tall as trees with arms and legs as big around as your Father's chest. They live naked except for the tiger skins they tie around their waists and the metal rings they have forged around both ankles and wrists. An* oni's *grin is a most horrid sight for it is full of long and filthy fangs and holds the certainty that there is nothing in the forest that can defeat it. On every* oni's *foul head jut two horns just visible through their mass of wiry, muck-filled hair. Their eyes bulge like two rice bowls turned upside down and their brows furrow deep with bitterness.*

The only difference between oni *is their color. Some wear their leather-like skin in the palest blue, a color so shocking that when one of the beasts leaps from behind a tree with its mass of white hair sticking up at all ends, snarling like a mad wolf, you gasp and take to run only to find he has got you by the nape of the neck.*

The second type remains hidden in the shadows with its deep maroon-colored skin. It waits until you creep almost on top of it. You'll notice first its rotten stench and then its hungry breath as it gusts into your face. By then you are so close that when your eyes adjust to take in its size your knees give out. That kind of oni *doesn't even have to work for its meal, doesn't even have to lower its spike-studded club from its great shoulder.*

Did you know there are children who, after hours of being gnawed, still sit in the terrific heat of an oni's *belly wishing they had only been good?*

We were all very careful to obey any and all of Grandma's rules.

That day we knew there wouldn't be any merriment with our sham *oni* until we had completed our chores; and more worrisome, until Father came back. He had set off several days before to visit Tanioku Town. It was a trip he made every four or five months and always before *setsubun*. Grandma insisted on sardines as a part of her ritual and the town was the only place he could obtain them. Apart from the fish, he also stocked up on oil and sugar and—I learned eventually—the candies and sweets he'd later shower us with.

Outside we marveled at the fat low-belly of a sky and the shiver of something electric in the air. Jiro jumped up and down, sweeping his fingers against the fog.

"This is just weird," he said, taunting the foreboding gloom.

"The ground tickles." Sui shuffled her bare feet, occasionally rubbing the soles up and down her dirty calves.

"Let's get going," I said.

The weather held out long enough for us to finish our work and gather the holly that Grandma had asked for. It was almost nightfall when we got in, cleaned up, and sat down for dinner.

"You didn't see your father out there did you?" Mother asked, clearly agitated.

"No," I said. "I'm sure he'll be in before the rain hits."

"Here, you need to tie these to the front door and the gate and walk down to the pass to see if you spot him," said Grandma. "It's getting late. We need those sardines."

It was then that I noticed that the evening's meal was unusually sparse.

"The heads?" I asked.

"We'll do that when he gets in," she said. "Hurry up, or someone will eat your rice."

I secured some bundles of holly to the front door and set about decorating both sides of the gate when I pricked myself with one of the waxy leaves. I saw that I had drawn blood and dropped the rest of the plant. *The rain is going to wash it all away anyway*, I thought. Besides it didn't feel right. My favorite part was skewering dozens of crinkled black sardine heads—cooked until

their eyes glazed milky white—and using them for further decoration on the fence. Mere holly didn't seem to hold the same
power. I was sure Grandma agreed.

The storm would hit any minute now, the air was tense and
full with the faint, near constant rumbling of thunder. I looked
out over the flat fields that rose into foothills and finally into the
Kiri Naki Mountain range, but caught no sight of Father. I was
less worried about his safety—this wouldn't be the first time he'd
spend the night holed up in some cave waiting for the weather to
pass—than I was dejected about missing the excitement of bean
throwing and devils and candies.

Sucking my pierced thumb, I turned to head back home. That's
when it happened.

In a shriek of exploding white I saw the maple tree split and
splinter, felt its icy wooden chunks pelt my back and leave sting-
ing trails across my prickling, sickly, screaming skin. The worm
of nausea heaved my stomach, and I calmly observed the passing of the single thought, *Sure glad I didn't eat dinner yet.* I'm pretty
sure I was smiling for that long ink-black moment when I tum-
bled free, totally conscious of the fact that this time there were
no hands to save me.

Sometime afterwards, flown and twisted, there was solely the
weight of the earth pushing up, the sky behind me no longer
interested. Bewildered. I was lead back by the insistent hissing in
my dreamy ears ultimately giving way to a pitiful moaning that in
time—as I clawed my way to the surface—I realized was coming from me.

I danced on my unsteady feet, raised my fist to the sky.

"Missed me."

That might have been it, the moment. I've witnessed enough
living and dying to believe now that it only takes one sin, one
sin too many, to overwhelm the bowl of luck, causing it to tip.
When it rocks upright again, it is all but empty. I've seen it over
and over. And I sometimes think that might have been my one-
sin-too-many. *Missed me*—never tease the gods.

My ears continued their tormenting whine until they were
cleared by a single howl falling off of Kiri Naki Mountain. I

turned in a circle, following the echo as it leapt from hill to hill. Instead of ending, however, it was picked up by another lament, and another; and then, encouraging the goose flesh on my arms, the howl turned to laughter.

In the distance the sky broke loose, caving to the rush of sheet rain running across the land. It was coming for me. On half-melted legs I hurried back up the path, imagining a hasty advance of a thousand angry footsteps behind me.

"Did you see him?" Rubbing both arms, Mother walked down the hall, probably to see what was taking me so long or to investigate the lightening strike. I slammed the front door and locked it. Just then the rain struck our tiled roof in a clatter and I cried out.

My head wasn't straight. The question wasn't right. *Did you see him? Him? Didn't she mean them?*

"Father?" she said. "Is he coming? Did you see his light in the trees?"

I shook my head, helpless to the shudder building inside me and trying not to remember the lights I had seen in the trees, an army of them, all much larger than Father's torch, all marching down the mountains with amazing speed, ripping out brush and trees in their stampede.

There was no dinner for me that night, no chewy rice cakes to savor, not even a cup of hot tea to remove the chill. Before anything could be heated, Shime toddled to the corner of the room and pointed up at the god shelf that Grandma kept decorated with sake, water, and salt. It was vibrating.

"The devil's gate," Grandma gasped.

Every house has a point that sits in the most northeastern direction. This spot is called the *kimon* or devil's gate. Ever since I was a small child and Grandma caught me stealing sips of sake, she tried to impress on me its importance. *It's where the devils most easily slip into the house*, she used to say. *If you defile it, you invite them into your home. They'll come at night while you're dreaming and rend you to shreds.* Once again scared witless by Grandma's stories, I stole my sake from Grandpa's bottle from then on.

Ornaments on the shrine began to rattle, topple, the tall vase smashed to the floor, water fingering its way across the tatami mat. Shime ran into my arms, her warm breath on my neck calmed me. I knew what was coming.

"We have to hide," Grandpa said.

Jiro and Sui knelt in the bottom of the empty bathtub. One by one the babies were handed down. Shime clasped my shirt when it was her turn. But I couldn't go in with her. At eleven I was no longer considered a child. Inside we stuffed towels and old blankets to muffle the screaming. Shime looked up at me with anxious eyes, but she still did not cry.

"Quiet, quiet," Jiro begged, rocking one of the twins. I touched one of Shime's curls and replaced the cover we used over the bathtub to keep the water hot.

The shaking grew until the entire house swayed and the thin frames of the *shoji* doors popped in two. A constant rumbling, like a peal of thunder that refused to break, could be heard growing all around us. It was then I noticed the stench of deep earth, almost sour in my mouth and that some of them were carrying drums. *They're close*, I thought.

Back in the main room Grandma sat in fervent prayer at the altar while Grandpa was nowhere to be seen. Mother beckoned me from a futon closet. There we hid, pressed tight between the heavy, mold-scented mats, acutely aware of our wild heartbeats, sure they would give us away.

The moment the monsters reached our house was the worst. Except for the rain droning outside, there was silence. The house was still. I thought they might have gone and poked my head out from the futons. That is when I heard them. They were circling the house, sniffing, dragging their giant clubs through the mud, and grunting among themselves. I could make out the rattle in their chests and the explosive exhales of disgust at not finding what they were looking for.

And then it happened, a solitary beastly wail tore through the silence and a second later the house jumped. It sounded as if half a wall had been torn away. I could hear the pretty blue tiles breaking loose and sliding off the roof to shatter in the wet dirt. I imagined the *oni gawara*, the tile that had received so many prayers, falling and being crushed beneath some enormous thick-soled foot leaving us even more unprotected.

All at once the rest joined in and began to roar, deep guttural cries of excitement, as they beat their drums and swung their clubs in celebratory devastation.

The rest is fragments, feathers of thin memory: the stink of filthy animal skin, the fatty acrid smoke that bellowed from the torches that burned despite the rain. Crying and praying and the icy downpour that blurred my vision and numbed my skin.

And then they were gone.

Father never did return from his trip. It took Grandma one month to sew the proper amulets and instill in each of us her most potent charms. An hour's worth of chanting and she dissembled the family altar and fastened it to my back. We took as much as we could carry and left everything else behind. It wasn't until we reached Tanioku Town that we learned Father had never even arrived.

Afterwards, Jiro didn't speak another word and Grandpa drank a little more than usual. The rest of us shouldered a kind of blanket exhaustion that only people who have lived briefly in hell understand. It happens when the story is much too vivid and true to tell.

I often think about the real hero that night. Sui. When the *oni* tore down the wall and peeled back the top of the wooden bathtub the children all cried out. It was Sui, though, who all at once understood why they were there. She gripped Shime tight to her chest, cursing and spitting, and refusing to let go. When they pulled Sui up by one leg and shook it so badly that the bones ground to a fine powder (to this day it is useless and she has never married), she kicked with her other leg and held fast to our good luck baby. Of course she was no match; she couldn't win. And in the end the *oni* got exactly what they wanted, their baby back.

tip of the nose

"Sumimasen." Mi bowed low to the businessman who bumped past her only to fall into the last empty seat on the train. She held the bow a moment longer, pressing her purse and shopping bag neatly against her stomach, letting a group of high school kids jump in. A boy wearing a pair of pants that desperately needed a belt clipped her shoulder.

"Watch it!"

She wanted to curse the teen, but didn't. For as long as she could remember, Mi was certain that other people could hear her thoughts. Mostly, this made her painfully timid, but on occasion it roused an apprehension that escalated in leaps. Profuse sweating, hyperventilating, and what until that day she thought was the final step—a funny tic that heaved her shoulder to her ear, and snapped her head down to meet it. The headache that followed.

It was Wednesday, hospital day, and she was on her way home from visiting her grandmother-in-law in the city. The old woman never knew she was there. It made Mi a little jealous, actually. Sitting there, stroking the tiny, corded hand and imagining how happy the old woman must be, how enlightened, beyond worry of family, money, and bodily functions. If it just didn't take so much living to get there, she thought.

Today Mi was late. She had dallied too long at the vegetable vender. There was a sale, one hundred yen off anything that grew on a vine. With two packs of strawberries in her hands, she debated if lotus root was considered a climber and missed her usual bus. As a result, she missed her usual train as well.

Now, begging to dissolve under the fluorescent lights, Mi read over and over the advertisement for Hamanako Boat Racing, trying to keep her mind off how much she truly disliked the people who rode the 8:45.

Two years ago Mi's mother-in-law declared that she would no longer observe hospital day. However, if Mi would go instead, she could probably find time to watch her six grandchildren—but for no more than three hours, once a week. Mi didn't want to leave the house. It was only there, sunk and swollen in the daily commotion, that she found her head seemed to be completely unreadable. It was not so friendly outside.

But her grandmother-in-law had always been a kind woman and would soon reside in the family altar bestowing graces of health and good fortune to those she felt fit. It was the least that Mi could do.

Dressed in clothes that hadn't fit her properly in years, she kissed each child on the forehead, checked her purse for a freshly ironed handkerchief, a package of tissues, and at least enough money for train and bus fare; she then kissed each child again, this time on the cheek.

The beltless boy was arguing loudly on his mobile phone. To make his point he held the device low and slapped the floor of the train with one hand. Mi winced.

Reading advertisements only worked for so long. It was time for more efficient methods. She began repeating to herself, *tip of the nose, tip of the nose, tip of the nose . . .*

In elementary school she had met a Buddhist priest; this was back when she was less shy—somewhat of a tomboy—before her head opened up. She asked the man what he thought about sitting there all day with his hands in his lap. The bald man laughed, patted her on the knee and explained how he held his attention on the tip of his nose, the air coming in, the air going out. He added that on a good day, he didn't think about anything at all.

Mi adopted the practice years later and found that for the most part it worked. At the end of the day, up to her neck in bathwater that had already embraced seven other family members and was no longer very hot, she would kid herself about her Buddhist bent and fantasize that maybe one day she might just stumble into enlightenment herself. And then all this pain would vanish.

A nasal voice announced the next station. The train slowed, then stopped and most of the passengers, including the ill-behaved high school boys, got off. A few boarded and a whistle blew. Mi moved to an empty cushioned bench and sat down. She flattened the pleats of her skirt, adjusted the shopping bag and her purse in her lap. She looked at her watch and thought (a safe thought) that she had less than an hour before she would be home. She dared to wonder if her eldest and youngest would be asleep, when she heard someone coming down the aisle. *Click, click, click.*

It couldn't be! Her thought was obviously too loud because the blind man who skipped his cane back and forth across the floor stopped abruptly in front of her and took a seat on the adjacent bench.

She squirmed. *Tip of the nose, tip of the nose . . .*

The man who sat in front of her was her age, thick black-and-gray hair, long and tied back into a ponytail. His T-shirt, one size too small, stretched tight to reveal his broad chest and shoulders. His upper arms were soft muscle as well. With giant hands he held his cane, eyes closed, his head tilted slightly as if he were listening for something. He was as handsome as ever.

Mi jumped at the thought. She began to fidget, twisting the strap of her purse one way and then the other. *So he did go blind?*

The story Mi had heard during her childhood was that when Tada was born, he was visited by his great aunt, a blind woman who even strangers approached for advice. It was said that when she took him into her arms she briefly regained her sight and later recalled not only the fine weave of her sister's kimono, but also the pattern of the infant's blanket and the depth to which her brother's hair had receded. Wiping off the tears that fell onto the baby's cheeks, she apologized and announced that the child too would lose his sight. It was a prediction that was never doubted despite Tada being a normal boy for the seventeen years that Mi knew him.

She stared at the man in front of her all the while feeling her breath lurch higher in her chest, becoming less and less effective. Her lips moved, *tip of the nose, tip of the nose.* With extreme effort Mi took a deep breath. *In, one-two-three; hold, one-two-three; out, one-two-three.* She did it again. A little longer.

Mi hated the number four, *shi*, the same pronunciation for the word death. She managed to avoid it whenever possible. Never setting the microwave on any time that began or ended with the number, never purchasing only four items of anything, and if she had the unfortunate luck to be rung up with a total that included *shi*, Mi did not hesitate to put something back, two items if necessary. She took the count directly to five. Her eyes crossed looking at the very end of her nose, eyelids half shut, and she began. Slowly inhaling, *one-two-three-four-five . . .*

There was a very brief moment when she reached five and the previously unseen battle that had been waging between her gray tweed skirt and about twenty-five centimeters of black thread, exhausted by too many years of laundry and sun, ended. The button on the side of her skirt made a ridiculously loud pop, shot into the air, and landed with a plastic tinkle as it rolled down the length of the car.

Mi's head hit her shoulder hard, her faced burned. Gulping breaths in shallow catches, her head and shoulder collided again and she squeezed the plastic bag in her lap. Mi was terrified of doing something even more embarrassing when she was saved at the last minute by the smell of overripe strawberries bursting—a cool stain across her stomach and down her leg, filling her shoe.

She squatted on the soft earth plucking weeds from the sandy soil and tossing them into the bamboo basket strapped to her back. Tada had just finished mending a large tear in the plastic hot house and already the temperature had risen enough to pull plump drops of sweat from her brow. Ever since she started helping out at his grandparents' strawberry farm, Mi liked to pretend the candy-sweet smell had the power to intoxicate. First as an explanation for her giddiness or maybe just an excuse to act silly, but soon she came to believe it. For a long time after, even when she hadn't seen Tada for years, just the faintest waft of cheap potpourri would make her swoon.

"Let's take a break." Tada pulled the basket off of her aching shoulders and handed her his thermos full of cold wheat tea.

"Arigatou." Mi planted her bottom on a damp furrow, letting her legs splay and absent-mindedly wiping her hands on her slacks. If her mother had been there she would certainly have delivered a slap upside the head. But she wasn't there. Mi giggled at the thought. Tada dropped a handful of berries on his spread-out handkerchief and opened a tin of condensed milk. He chose the biggest strawberry, blew on it lightly, and then swirled it in the sticky syrup.

"Say ahhh."

They had always been inseparable, by default: a combination of proximity and the vague oddness that repelled the other children. Over time their play turned to talk, silences that were easy, and finally this new place where they suddenly kept secrets. They were always together.

But it wasn't until then—mud-caked knees and fingernails full of sand; sweat tickling down her back; and a head fuzzy-full of strawberry air—that Mi realized she loved him. Less than a minute later, when he wiped her chin with his warm fingers, she decided he was the man she would marry.

The squeak of the train's brakes woke Mi from the past. The hard lean to the right rolled her onto her side and off the seat. The crack of her knee on the floor was disguised by the conductor announcing the next stop and reminding the passengers not to leave anything behind.

Gathering herself, placing her bags and purse in the crook of her elbow and holding her skirt together with the other hand, she noticed that Tada was already at the doors, now opening.

Mi hobble-hopped off the train so deep in her tip-of-the-nose mantra that she recognized neither the button that snapped under her foot or the fact that her stop was still two stations away. Somehow she managed to retrieve her ticket from an ill-supported pocket, hand it to the station attendant, and pass through the turnstile before it struck her where she was.

"Home," she said under her breath.

It was true. From the time she was born until the day her family hastily moved to a nearby town, this had been her home.

Mi watched Tada make his way down the covered arcade, the cane swinging back and forth, the pedestrians walking large semicircles around him. His back, broad and slightly hunched, was familiar to a part of her she once loved. Her chest burned.

Mi's body suddenly hiccough-sobbed so violently that she momentarily lost her grip on the two pieces of tweed. No one seemed to notice the skirt slide down over the satin slip or how the undergarment bunched up over the waistline when she yanked it back into position and threatened it under her fist. No one saw either while she examined the magnificent bloom that dyed her white cotton shirt pink or when she wiped tears away with the back of her hand because the pain cut so hard in her knee that it buckled when she placed too much weight on it.

"I just want to go home," Mi said to no one at all.

The clock on the tower showed 9:50. Through a series of whistles and buzzes she heard the train leave the station behind her. There wouldn't be another for at least twenty minutes. By the time she got back her mother-in-law would be furious and her husband would be in from work wondering why the bath wasn't drawn, no less angry but waiting for his mother to leave before he let on. It would probably take twenty minutes to buy another ticket and make it back to the platform.

Mi set her bags down for a moment, wanting to smooth her hair. However, with one hand still firmly gripping the side of her skirt, she could not properly gather the wild strands and tame them with the tricky barrette and so she ended up tossing it aside. She scooped back up the bags and tested her knee, finding that if she walked with it completely straight, she could at least move without collapsing or crying out.

Tada had turned the corner at the end of the street and was out of sight. It was okay, though. She knew exactly where to go. She followed slowly, one stiff leg thrusting her body one way, riding the swing back only to be kicked near sideways again. There was some kind of speed to the momentum, and how it fit so well with the ever playing song in her head, *tip-of-the-nose-tip-of-the-nose* . . . It took over now, even relieving much of the pain.

The covered arcade was lined on both sides with shops, only a few she recognized. Old Man Kurimoto's coffee house was still there, no doubt run by one of his four sons, and the tea kettle store remained, as dusty and faded and free of window shoppers as ever. But mostly there were bars.

There were hostess clubs that boasted an all-foreign staff, karaoke lounges where both the music and the customers occasionally spilled out into the street, and dark doorways where young Japanese men stood in fancy suits thumbing their mobile phones.

Mi continued to the end of the street, turning down a darker, narrower road lined with small yardless houses. She couldn't see as well, but it was quieter and she could make out the click of Tada's cane.

Before she turned at the next block she had already promised herself she would not look at her old home. This she could not do. And she almost made good on that promise except for one thing. Halfway down the block, standing outside Tada's house after watching him go inside, Mi let slip a mumbled tip-of-the-nose and accidentally surprised a large sleeping dog on the steps of the house next door, her old home.

The dog woke and barked and lunged at her so quickly her immediate response was to scream and run. Unfortunately, her bad knee was no better and she collapsed to the ground. The dog continued to yelp but was stopped from reaching her by an extremely short leash.

Mi lay on the ground, observing the creature, deciding after a bit that she wasn't afraid. This dog lived its entire life knotted to the end of a fraying rope and despite that he still had an opinion. It wasn't pity but admiration she felt. She only wished she could get up.

It wasn't long that she lay there, her hair matted with sweat on her forehead and cheeks, her hands and elbows bleeding, and two packages of strawberries and her purse pinned flat under an enormous hip. Her dog-friend continued to express himself until the door to Tada's house slid open.

"Who's there?" he asked.

Tip-of-the-nose-tip-of-the-nose . . .

"Who is it?" Tada came out and stood over Mi. "Pochi, shut up, will you?"

The dog quieted with a final growl and lay back down in the one position it could manage.

"Thank you," Tada said to the animal. "Now what are you doing down there?"

"Me? Oh, the dog just frightened me. I think I twisted my knee, but I'm fine."

Tada said nothing.

"If you could just call a taxi for me. I'll be on my way." She expected it to work.

"Mi-chan?" he asked.

"I'm sorry . . ."

"What are you doing here? How did you get here? Are you okay?" Tada squatted and found her hand. "What happened? I thought you—I tried to find you. I asked everyone." He moved so that he could pull her into a half-sitting position in his lap. He petted her hair. Using an index finger, he gently moved the tangles away from her face.

"I'm so sorry, Tada. It's all my fault." Mi was crying freely now. "They knew. Somehow they knew. They took me away and made me—"

Everything was home. The inflection in his voice, the warmth of his skin, even the fragrance of strawberries and displaced earth was right there between them.

Tada squeezed her tight and buried his face in her mussed-up hair.

"There was a baby then?" he said, his voice faltering

"Yes." Mi held tight to his arm. "Somehow they knew. Father—" Tada rocked her and stroked her hair. Although he didn't make a sound, she felt his tears meet hers and run down her neck.

When her sobbing subsided she lay in the vast thrum of exhaustion. It felt as if a long nagging worry had suddenly vanished. Her torrent of thoughts stilled. Tada, eyes closed, his face so near she could smell the familiar taste of his mouth. With quivering fingertips he traced the arch of her eyebrows, the curve of her jaw. He moved some hair behind her ear and lay the cool back of his hand against her forehead like a mother checking a child for a fever.

"I missed you," he said. "I didn't think I would survive."

"Me, too."

"Can we fix this?" he asked.

"Yes," Mi said. "We can."

She wished she could stay like this forever, lying entirely relaxed against the strong curve of her old lover's body. She looked up at him adoring the silhouette of his nose, the plumpness of his lips. Bravely, she made a wish. And then it dawned on her, her mind was unreadable. Mi smiled and felt her chest swell. From now on she would have places in her head to tuck away a secret or two. And then right there on the ground wrapped in Tada's arms, Mi dared to dream up as many secrets as she possibly could.

Eden on the 18th floor

Obon, The Festival For the Dead— August

One month after Old Mr. Mutoh's wife passed away, one year before he would follow, his children took a secret vote. Tradition favored that he should be left alone; and then only after the grieving should he be asked to live with his eldest son Taiki and his wife. Instead it was Taiki who broke the news, sold the land, the house, and moved the old man into the city—all without a single word of consultation.

Clothes were boxed, books tied into neat stacks. His daughter-in-law spent an entire afternoon kneeling in front of the *butsudan*-altar curling yesterday's *Asahi Newspaper* around candles, their holders, the bowl-shaped bell and its heavy wooden stand. When she came upon the framed black-and-white picture of his deceased wife, she asked if the old man might want to carry it in his lap for the car ride. Mr. Mutoh thought that was a good idea. He thought she might enjoy the drive over thread thin roads that boxed in rice fields and mikan orchards, roads that grew fat and paved through the town that didn't even have a train station when they were children or a convenience store when they were married.

It took four hours for one truck and one minivan to enter the Tokyo sprawl and arrive at the slate grey, twenty-story apartment. The characters down the side read GREEN FORREST TOWER.

A too-friendly sort of man sporting a greasy cowlick that looked suspiciously on-purpose and a pale blue suit complete with tangerine-colored tie herded the three of them into the elevator, explaining that he was giving them the tour of the facilities. Brand new, grand opening held just this past June and already at eighty percent occupancy.

Despite insistence from his son, the old man chose not to leave the photograph in the car. He cradled it in both arms against his chest. Only once did he bashfully cover his wife's eyes—for the three floors they were joined by a group of high school girls in sailor uniforms, their skirts rolled at the waist. That and the mini socks barely peeking out over the rims of their Kiltie loafers stretched their long legs even longer. Mr. Mutoh didn't care to think about what so much nakedness might do to his wife's weak constitution.

"Your room is on the 18th floor, number 1878." Their greasy guide read from a small square of metal he pulled from his pocket. "That should be easy enough to remember, don't you think?"

"Hm," Mr. Mutoh answered.

"Is that the key?" Reiko, the old man's daughter-in-law, pointed at the metal piece. She giggled, covering her mouth.

"Why, yes it is." Cowlick Man handed it over for her to examine.

"Oh, dad, look at this. Isn't it fascinating? This is what a key looks like in the big city. This is what you'll use to open your door." Reiko had a child's voice, a slight lisp that owed less to genetics or anatomy and more to her penchant for preteen romance manga. It made her sound so infuriatingly dim, it had to be an act.

"Won't fit on my key chain." The old man blew air through his nose. He couldn't even remember the last time he had locked the door on the farm. He didn't even own a key chain.

Taiki, Reiko, and the Pastel Man all laughed at the joke.

A melodic *ding* swallowed the air around them and then the elevator doors swished open.

Several minutes were spent explaining, demonstrating, and then practicing the front lock before the slimy man stepped into the apartment, out of his shoes, and into a pair of waiting slippers. He threw out one hand and read flawlessly from the script in his head.

"Here it is, Green Forrest Tower's pride and joy, the Single

Man's Dream—The Silver Series." He made a clucking sound with his tongue and aimed two quick jabs at Mr. Mutoh with his elbow. The old man jumped at the gesture and moved away. "I'm sure you can appreciate how convenient it will be to have your kitchenette, toilet, and bath all connected to your living/bedroom. But before I show you anything, I noticed you're not alone." The man nodded at the picture. "I think you're both going to love this."

The three of them followed him down a narrow hall and into a perfectly square room.

"Tadah!" he sang out as he opened the doors to a small closet. "This is the family altar room. You'll find your *butsudan* fits comfortably inside. The doors can be kept open during the day, while you're at home. And then shut at night or when you go out. It keeps the dust down." The baby blue–suited man demonstrated by opening and closing them several times.

"You see, studies have shown that a good many precious ornaments have been broken by well-intentioned elderly folk trying to polish them. And you never know, there might also be a time when you have a house guest, and you don't want her to see the altar, the beloved wife looking down on you and all." Mr. Apricot Tie made the jabbing motion again.

"I'll be leaving the doors open," the old man said, shifting the picture in his arms. "Thank you."

ONE MONTH LATER—
GREEN FORREST TOWER, ROOM 1878

The old man knelt in front of the *butsudan*, and through a fuzzy string of sandalwood incense, spoke with his wife. It was five in the afternoon and he was sharing his evening meal with her. They always ate together. The rice, fish, miso soup, even the green tea had been divided and placed into separate bowls. He crowded the nicer set of dishes on the altar and because he had no appetite, he sat with his chopsticks in his soup, slicing the cubes of tofu in half and then in half again.

He was telling her how afraid he was, not of being alone or

being in a strange place, not even of the loud and smelly city. He explained that it was the *shini-gami*, the God of Death that really spooked him. He said he felt it gnawing at him, mostly around his neck and ears, and that sometimes he woke up at night pinned facedown on his pillow with the *shini-gami*'s crushing weight on the back of his head.

Mr. Mutoh then changed the subject. He asked if his wife got to see Daisuke and Hanae, the two children they had lost. Daisuke would have been their eldest son, except he didn't make it past the second trimester. Hanae, their little girl, was stricken with a fever that buried her three days before her first birthday.

There had been his best friend since grade school and the boating accident. War buddies, the children on the islands that helped him catch and kill wild pigs . . . others. These last few years it seemed like every other month or so some friend, neighbor, or relative was dying. He didn't understand why he was left. Maybe because he was good at taking care of things.

But it wasn't until his wife's *otsuya* after everyone had gone home and he lay half asleep in the freezing room patting her lifeless hand that the game became clear. Death, he understood now, had a plan. With long, methodical strokes it was taking away everyone he had ever cared about, starting from his own mother who died in childbirth.

It wasn't bad luck, fate, or the curse that more than a few sighted people warned him about. It was a vicious *shini-gami* content to scratch away at his sanity. Until he himself crumbled, it would take everyone, but him. The old man confided in his wife, he wasn't afraid to die. He was afraid not to.

But again she disagreed.

The old man looked around this new world he lived in. So this was it. The Single Man's Dream—The Silver Series. It was a box with walls painted a white that gave him headaches and a ceiling that was so high it made him nervous. The stove didn't actually get hot, but his water boiled. The refrigerator had a dozen drawers and doors—each with a secret. One kept ice, one ice cream, another held vegetables in an environment that actually increased their vitamin content over time, while still another kept his *sashimi* almost frozen yet perfectly sliceable. Any drawer or

door left open for more than sixty seconds would send the appli-
ance into fits of beeping until it was closed again. He realized
it took him exactly sixty seconds to make his way back across
the room and lower himself into a comfortable position on the
floor.

The toilet was dangerous as well. Colored buttons and dials
lined the side with tiny pictures he could not quite see. Pushing
himself up three days ago, he set off a water jet that shot warm
liquid all up his back. When he attempted to turn it off, the water
turned into a cool mist before it eventually huffed hot puffs of air
into his face. As a final insult a woman's voice echoed from the
porcelain bowels and wished him a very good day.

For as small as the place was, it continued to surprise and more
often than that embarrass him. It was a week after he moved in
before he realized he even had a veranda. Taiki had opened the
thick beige curtains and disappeared.

"Dad! Have you seen this?"

The old man followed his son through the sliding glass doors.
One step brought him flush against the chest-high wall. Far
below him and far above, Tokyo-gray stretched out to merge
in an indistinct smog that settled on the horizon. Wherever he
looked in any direction, buildings jutted from the ground at different rates of growth.

"Isn't that beautiful?"

"The most beautiful sight I've ever seen," Mr. Mutoh said.
He was reminded of bones. Not pink ones that thumped with
breath, not even the singed fragments that were his wife's; the
ones that only two months earlier he had plucked from the pile
of ash and passed from chopstick to chopstick, from child to
child and finally to urn. He didn't know why he thought of
bones. Heat threatened his eyes. In order to see the street below,
to change his thoughts, he stepped up on an air conditioner hose
and leaned farther over the rail.

"Careful there." Taiki slipped a finger through one of his
father's belt loops. "We don't want to have any accidents, now
do we?"

"So where is this green forest everyone is talking about?"

"What?" Taiki took a moment. He was not their smartest

child. "Oh, Dad. That's just a name. I am pretty sure there is a park close by, though. I'll look up the subway lines and the bus schedules for you."

The old man snorted the only way he knew how and went back inside.

LATE SEPTEMBER—
GREEN FORREST TOWER, ROOM 1878

When the doorbell rang a small monitor on the wall next to the light switch showed a video image of whoever was outside. Mr. Mutoh was now standing examining a face he had never seen before. He mumbled to himself.

"Who is it? Who is it?"

"I have a package," came the scratchy answer.

The old man used the wall for support. "You can hear me?" he whispered into the device.

"Yes, I can and I have a package here. Will you open the door? It's heavy."

Ten minutes later Mr. Mutoh stood in the middle of the room next to a large box. The picture on the front resembled a stroller, but instead of a crib for a baby it had a low, cushioned seat. Attached to hinges, it could be lifted to reveal a deep compartment. The old man knew what it was. Back home they called them *silubaa guruma* or silver cars. They were popular among the elderly, the men and women who had weak legs, crooked backs or wandering minds. These were the people who had long since stopped working the fields and spent their days pushing *silubaa guruma* to the vegetable markets. There they'd tuck bags of hairy *sato imo*, lacy *maitake* mushrooms and red-skinned sweet potatoes into the seat. They'd park semi circle under a shade tree and spend half the afternoon complaining about their children, neighbors, and their most recent numbness or pain.

The card attached to the box was signed by his youngest daughter, Ai, the one who lived in Hokkaido and didn't get down much. It read: Dear Dad, Hope you enjoy your Healthy Walker. See you soon, Ai.

It wasn't his fault he got lost last week. It was impossible to navigate without a horizon, without even the vaguest idea of where the sun might sit in the sky, and as if to further sway the odds against him, there were far too many people. Great hordes gathered at the intersections, all apparently invisible to each other, for no one said hello when they brushed shoulders on the curb or excuse me when they collided in the streets. But what made the old man feel most uneasy, feel most like he was the only living soul among so many hungry ghosts, was that no one dared to even make eye contact.

He didn't have a chance. He took a sidelong glance at the picture of his wife above the altar.

"Looks like someone is trying to get me to exercise. Ha!"

After removing the Healthy Walker from the box, he hauled it out to the veranda. Despite the overhang of a roof, he sincerely hoped it would rust.

Ohanami, Cherry Blossom Viewing— Early April—Ueno Park

The three of them sat on a large blue plastic sheet. On all four sides, other families lounged on their sheets, beyond them more families, more sheets. At regular intervals, great bushy cherry trees stood with bent limbs shedding their pale petals over the crowd.

Someone in the distance had a karaoke machine hooked up to a generator. Two drunken businessmen with arms draped heavily around each other's necks sang "My Way" to what looked like their entire office. The sun was already low in the sky; still everyone ate and drank, laughed or slept, each rectangle of plastic a world impenetrable by its neighbors.

Reiko kneeled at the low table and stacked lacquered *obento* boxes. Taiki rolled onto his side and using a folded *zabuton* cushion as a pillow, closed his eyes. The old man stood to stretch his legs. He staggered. It had been quite some time since he had had this much to drink.

"You okay there?" Reiko asked in her darling voice.

"Cramp. Fine."

"Sure you didn't have a little too much to drink?" She giggled, stood, and smoothed her skirt. "I think I did. I'm going to find the little girl's room." Slipping on her shoes she maneuvered her way through the blue plastic islands.

"Humph," the old man said as she left. He was just about to sit down and have another cup of sake. He had decided that morning if he was lucky, either his liver would fail or his kidneys would blow. If not he would just have to settle with a well-timed fall on the way home.

Something caught his eye.

Darting above the oblivious picnickers, through the showers of petals, flew a single dragonfly. It had a thick body, yellow and black stripes. Briefly it circled a couple sitting a few sheets away. The woman swung at it with one hand, the other holding a thin stick skewered with sweet *mochi* balls. Her attention was on pulling them off one by one with her teeth. The old man felt his jaw go loose. This was no ordinary dragonfly. This was an *Oniyanma*! A Tiger Spiketail! Not only was it rare, it was practically unseen these days. Indeed, he thought there weren't anymore left! He looked around the park. No one else seemed to recognize what a marvelous creature flew so close. Even the children refused to interrupt their games of tag to look up.

This is impossible, he told himself. *Here it is April.* He did the math. *The fly season doesn't start until June. And the* Oniyanma*'s habitat is mountainous, not here, not this dirty city.* He squinted, trying to find some hill from which it might have descended.

"Everything okay, Dad?" Reiko was back.

"Fine, just thought I saw someone I knew." He rubbed his wet palms on his trousers.

"Here in Tokyo?" His daughter-in-law began to poke her husband awake.

The old man turned back to find the dragonfly was now hovering over a plate of *edamame* skins that lay on the table of the family next to them. The parents had taken their little girl to the swings earlier and had not returned. The old man gulped hard and extended his arm at a high angle, his index finger pointed straight. *Relax, relax*, he told himself. *No sudden movements.* He concentrated his finger into tiny circles. In front of him the *Oni-yanma* lifted, shot upwards. Out of the corner of his eye he saw Reiko whispering into her husband's ear, Taiki was pulling the pillow over his head. *Come on little fellow, come on . . .* The Tiger Spiketail hesitated at the tip of his finger, no doubt growing curious, then dizzy. It lighted. His hands trembling, his breath squeaking out of his lungs, the old man brought the creature down to eye level. *Magnificent. It must be nearly ten centimeters long.* With his other hand he moved up behind it and closed its wings. *There.*

When Mr. Mutoh looked around again, he saw Reiko obviously upset, her husband pressing a thumb to the place between his eyebrows and nodding. Once more he turned his back to them and squatted down. He looked around for anything that could be used as a container. Something they wouldn't suspect.

"Dad." It was Taiki's tired voice. "What are you doing over there?"

There was no choice. He held the bright mirror-green eyes up to his own and apologized. I'll be careful, he said. Gently he tucked the insect into his jacket pocket. He buttoned the top and cupped his hand over the tiny bulge.

"Yep, a lot of fun." Old Mr. Mutoh used his free hand to cover an exaggerated yawn. "Can I go home now?"

Taiki and Reiko looked at each other with blank expressions. "Sure, yeah, we should get going."

Not Quite Alone—
Green Forrest Tower, Room 1878

"Shitsurei Shimasu!"

The old man heard Reiko's baby-lisp come from inside the house. He stood quickly, brushed his clothes, and then slid through the glass door. The curtain rings ran fast to the end of the rail stopping just as the two entered the living/dining/kitchen room.

"Dad!" Taiki sounded concerned. "Is everything okay?"

"Yes, fine, everything is fine." Mr. Mutoh was suddenly aware that his hair was mussed up, unwashed for maybe a week, and that he had wet patches on both knees, elbows and his bottom. He tried to calm the hair with one hand, the other hand covering the moist elbow. Reiko stood staring at him with her head cocked to one side, mouth forming a small oval.

Mr. Mutoh let loose a loud guffaw at the thought that ran through his head. It was more like a joke; *let's hope they never reproduce.* It took his wife a few seconds to quiet him, reprimand him for his rudeness. He bowed a full forty-five degrees and apologized.

"Dad . . . ," Reiko said and then for lack of a more urgent thought. "I'll make tea."

"Well, haven't seen you in ages," the old man said.

"I told you I had to work in Kyushu for a few months. You remember, right?" Taiki looked over at his wife who was filling the kettle with water. "And Reiko can't drive. But she called you every day, right? You remember her calling you every day?"

The old man honestly could not remember whether she had called or not. But his wife told him he should say yes. Instead, he spoke in the direction of the kitchen. "I wouldn't put my hand on the eye if I were you. It heats up pretty quickly."

"Huh?" Reiko looked up, jerked her hand away.

"Nasty owie," the old man said.

"Nasty owie?" Taiki repeated. "Dad, are you feeling okay?"

"Fine. Haven't felt this good in months. Been getting plenty of exercise . . ."

"Yes, we saw the Healthy Walker in the *genkan*. It looked a little dirty. You must really be getting around town. I'll have to tell Ai," Reiko said.

"Not such a bad device, actually." Mr. Mutoh watched his son and daughter-in-law exchange a glance. "How's that tea coming?"

"Almost ready," she said. "Taiki, you need to offer Mother some incense. It's been a while."

"No, no, no. That's okay," the old man said.

"Why is the *butsudan* closed up?"

The old man didn't move. He waited for advice, but that didn't come either. All he could do was use the short time before the scream to think.

"What happened?!" Taiki opened the doors of the altar-room closet wide. The inside was empty. Even the picture of the deceased wife, his mother, had vanished.

"Oh, that, yeah, sent it all out for a cleaning."

"You don't send family altars out to be cleaned."

Reiko removed her hand from her mouth just long enough to mouth the word *scam?* at her husband.

"Where did you send it? What was the company's name?"

"You're getting all upset over nothing. It was here, Green Forrest, a service the building has. Called the . . ." Mr. Mutoh paused. "Dust Away for the Dearly Departed." He paused again and for good measure. "The Silver Series." He smiled as large and convincingly as he could.

"Dad, are you all right?" Reiko was now at his side.

"When did they take it? When did they say they'd bring it back?" his son continued.

"Taiki, this isn't right. Something isn't right," Reiko said. "Why would someone do this to an old man? That gold Buddha was worth . . . I should have been here, tried to come. I should have called more . . ."

At that exact moment, as if given some otherworldly cue, a giant beetle dove off the top of the beige curtains and with a couple dozen *click-click* beats of its wings made a safe, if clumsy, landing onto the young woman's head.

"*Gokiburi! Gokiburi!*" She shrieked and began a furious dancing and screaming routine.

"You've got roaches?" Taiki said as he tried to handle his spastic and screeching wife.

"Don't be stupid. It's a beetle." The old man was attempting to dodge the flailing arms and at the same time pluck the frightened insect from the wild woman's hair. "Don't hurt it."

Reiko continued to howl and thrash about. "Get it off, get it off! I can't breathe! I can't breathe!"

But before the old man could rescue it, Taiki untangled the creature and threw it to the ground. Not realizing she was free of the beast, Reiko continued her tantrum. And just as the insect righted itself, adjusted its wings and made to fly to the old man's shoulder, one slippered foot descended.

"You!" The old man fell to his knees beside the bug. "You killed him."

There was a second hesitation while Reiko processed what had happened.

"Eyuuuu!" She crumbled to the ground and began to shake her leg and howl.

"What is going on? What is this?" Taiki demanded.

"This," Mr. Mutoh said cradling the crushed carcass in his shaky palm. ". . . was Daisuke . . . your older brother."

After the two left it took a long moment for the echoes of Reiko's hysterical sobbing and the sting of Taiki's reproach to fall away. Remaining were only a quickly cementing silence and a mangled beetle in a curled and trembling hand.

The old man left the door unlocked. He left the lights on and let the kettle boil dry. When he felt the sun had slid far enough to stain the sky a sad pink, he carried his son outside.

The floor of the veranda had been filled with thirty-two bags of potting soil, sufficiently moistened and topped with exactly twenty-five squares of sod; roughly nineteen trips to and from the nursery three blocks away. Still there was too much gray and room for escape. This was remedied when the old man bought a thin-meshed net and taped it over the gaping hole that looked over the city below. Up it ran salmon-colored morning glories twisted in and out of white satin moonflowers. Pots and planters and even baskets and bowls filled with every imaginable flower were pushed into corners and sometimes stacked for lack of room. There were Persian Buttercups and Hardy Begonia, sprays of Baby's Breath and a line of headless tulips. A giant pink Oriental Lily with a creamy-yellow throat stood proudly beside a mass of deep-blue Floss Flower and a Lacecap Hydrangea bush that boasted only one magnificent bloom. One of every plant he could carry.

But what really made this small space his Eden were the creatures. It was on his second visit to the flower shop that Mr. Mutoh wandered into the backroom and discovered shelves full of fish and newts and beetles for sale to Tokyo children who had obviously no place to catch any of their own. It really wasn't difficult to pick out the ones he knew.

It started with the cherry blossom viewing and the dragonfly. He realized the insect was his wife long before he even reached room 1878. Much like she did in the old days she talked to him all the way home; told him he needed his hair trimmed, a closer shave, why didn't he stand up straight and why did the right side of his face sag like that? And just like the old days the man didn't need to answer. He wasn't lonely anymore.

Life proved even better the day he found Hanae, his little girl. While he was waiting for the lights to change, she came and rested on the Hydrangea that was tied to the seat of his Healthy Walker. She was unmistakable, black and yellow, a blush of blue and the red-orange eye spot on the upper side of her hind wing, an Old World Swallowtail. She loved her new home and spent her days flitting between the Daylilies and the Clump Verbena and back again.

His best friend, a dirty brown long-horned beetle, came back full of all his raunchy humor and cursing. Shaking his long antennae he could keep the old man up half the night laughing. Relatives tended to be cicada, a vast *min-min-min* or *jii-jii-jii* most of the day and night. Enough to drive an old man mad, he liked to think.

Near the end, he grew so fond of his new talent that he even collected a few souls he didn't quite know yet; a half-dozen ladybugs, three green tree frogs and a lazy blue-tongued skink who was content to nibble on leaf litter and not say a word.

Of course there was also his son, the one that had never been born, Daisuke, the shiny black Hercules Rhino beetle.

The old man carried his corpse to the far end of the veranda and laid it on the polished *hinoki* wood of the *butsudan* tilted against the wall. The black and white picture of his wife was tied to the clothes rail. A thick black and yellow striped moustache, the *oniyanma* dragonfly, lay dozing across her upper lip.

"Look what he did," the old man said positioning the beetle into the lap of the expensive Buddha statue. "I finally get everyone back, and he goes and starts taking them away again."

His wife quivered her wings, said nothing. And except for a failed burp of a tree frog even the others were suspiciously quiet.

"Little Daisuke," the old man's voice cracked. "I finally got to know him, a really good kid." Wet spilled from his eyes and ran cold down his cheek and neck.

"I listened to you. I tried. I brought them all back one by one. But it won't work. I can't have you all taken away again."

Just then the Tiger Spiketail left its place on the picture and flew to a shriveled morning glory.

Without a word his wife explained exactly how he could win this battle.

Soon After—Police Station

"How could this happen?" Taiki asked. Reiko had been taken away by the second ambulance on the scene. She was now in a hospital sleeping fitfully in a room with five other patients. When she wakes she won't quite remember why she is there. She'll eventually go home, but will no longer giggle anymore or talk with a lisp.

"Well, sir, as near as we can determine"—the middle-aged policeman paused for a moment—"he jumped."

"No, he would never do that. He must have fallen." Taiki shifted uncomfortably in the chair. "How do you know he didn't fall?"

"I guess, yes, that is always possible. But we have pretty much ruled it out. There are two things, actually."

"What are they?"

"The first is what our staff psychologist brought to our attention. You know how you or I or anyone else, when we're entering a house will take off our shoes, and then straighten them, turning them around so that when it is time to leave we can just step easily back into them."

"It's habit, yes."

"Well, we found a muddy footprint on the *butsudan*, showing that this is how he got over the veranda wall. But what was even more curious was that your father took the time to remove his slippers and line them up before going over the edge."

"Nothing strange there," Taiki said.

"Well, yes, but he lined them up neatly and facing the wrong way. We often find this in jumpers. They make the effort to tidy up before their exit, to remove their shoes or slippers, but they also know they aren't coming back. So they purposefully face them the wrong way."

"What's the other thing?"

"Other thing, yes." The police officer turned a few sheets of paper on his clipboard. "The other thing is a little more . . . We actually have several witnesses that were on the street when it happened."

"What do they know? How could they tell if he just didn't slip while trying to fix something? Catch one of those stupid bugs he loved so much."

"Yes, I agree it would be difficult to discern such a thing in general. But . . ." The policeman scratched an eyebrow.

"But what?" Taiki said.

"They all say that after tearing down the net, he stood for a moment on the edge. He leapt, and then he . . . flapped."

"Flapped?"

"Yes, his arms, all the way down. He sort of dove and then began flapping his arms. There is one witness who . . ." The policeman read the paper in front of him using a finger to under-line each word. "One person thought that he saw your father actually hover for a moment or two on the way down."

"Ridiculous."

"Yes, very ridiculous. I just thought I'd mention it since it was in the report," the policeman said.

"I see . . . ," Taiki said. "I guess I just can't believe it. But he was never the same after he lost mom."

"I know it is a truly awful thing. It's not your fault. This is quite common in the elderly, actually. Especially men who have been taken care of all their lives."

"And he was acting strange." Taiki continued. "I was away on business. I should have stayed in town."

"It's not your fault," the policeman repeated.

"Yes . . ."

"There is one more thing. I heard you mention your father liked, um, collected insects?" the police officer said. "I don't think it really matters." He flipped more pages.

"Go ahead."

"There was something unusual when we discovered the body. I was wondering if you might understand it."

"Yes?"

"The first men on the scene noted that when they found him they also found a large dragonfly."

"A what?"

"A dragonfly. It was quite big, over ten centimeters long I suppose. But what was peculiar was that it didn't fly away, even after Rescue came."

"It just sat there?" Taiki asked.

"Yeah, sort of attached to the back of your father's head."

the seed of the mistake

Masa was standing on the station platform two minutes before the last train would arrive, just enough time to grab a beer from the vending machine, guzzle it, and toss the empty can into the bin before the doors closed. That was the plan.

However, slightly buzzed and sprinting to catch the departing train, Masa was stopped by a large stranger who stepped in front of him.

"You would have made it," the stranger said.

"What?" Knowing he didn't have enough money for a taxi or a hotel room for the night, Masa felt the germ of rage as he listened helplessly to the conductor's final call and watched the last train pull away from the station. He then felt it wither when he glanced back at the creature standing directly in front of him.

Feet planted wide, arms barely able to cross in front of its enormous chest, stood an *oni*. It was unmistakable. The stranger's skin, tanned a leathery red, pulled into a tight smile that froze awkwardly on its face. There was no mistaking those teeth either, yellow and each one as big around as Masa's thumb.

"You would have made the train. That is, if I hadn't stopped you."

"Um, yes." Masa examined his feet, uncomfortable in the silence of the now deserted platform. He usually enjoyed a good tussle, courted them when he had a little extra energy to exhaust. But not tonight. He didn't need a fight that he was not only sure to lose, but might not even survive. He shivered under the unpleasant sting of copper-colored eyes, the heat that seemed to radiate off the stranger.

The *oni* spoke again. "I like that." Its voice was massive, yet controlled. The young man figured it was more used to roaring than gentle conversation.

"Excuse me?" Masa defied all his good sense and looked up.

"You had a choice, your regular train in your usual car or a can of cheap beer." The *oni* reached up and scratched its head near one of the thick, nubby horns. "You took the risk. You chose both. And you would have made it. You always make it, no matter how late you're running."

"Oh that?" Masa smiled nervously and stole another look at the stranger. *How long had this creature been watching him?*

The stranger was in his fifties, maybe older. It was hard to tell with *oni*. It looked respectable, though. Even its suit hung perfectly over its gigantic body, no rips or tears. *Tailored maybe?* And the *oni* didn't stink of gamey meat and fermented *natto*-beans like all the other ones Masa had met before. As a matter of fact, when the breeze turned the young man thought he caught the delicious fragrance of Armani's Acqua Di Gio.

Still it stood there, an unmoving tower pulling that unnatural grin. After several weighty seconds of silence the stranger reached over and with one giant hand ruffled Masa's hair.

"Come on, I'll buy you another drink." It pulled the young man close and draped its tree-like arm around his neck. "Call me Oyaji-Father," it insisted.

"I'm Masa," the younger man squeaked. He was terrified. He was flattered. *This stranger may be a mere* oni, Masa thought, *but it didn't seem like the kind of monster that would walk out on a sickly wife and its nine-year-old son.*

Masa's father hadn't been a particularly righteous man even before he emptied their savings account and ran off with a hostess named Kitten. Still, burdened since birth with a fragile disposition, Masa's mother missed him greatly. She handled the shock by spending the rest of her days weeping and refusing to eat the meals she spent all day preparing. It was like suddenly Masa had become half-transparent, and only occasionally would she notice him and muster the strength to nag him about grades, remind him that he needed a haircut, or that he should probably take a bath. With a life like that behind him, Masa wasn't surprised at all that it took so little effort to fall in love with this well-groomed, secret-hoarding beast. For it to become his hero even.

For three months the *oni* taught Masa its every secret, the first one being its second nickname, The Five O'Clock Shadow. The Five O'Clock Shadow was infamous, a thief that had been breaking into homes for twenty-five years now without so much as one eyewitness. A feat made more remarkable when you knew he performed most of his deeds in broad daylight, on occasion being so bold as to work when the streets were their busiest, five o'clock. Since no one had ever seen him, it was never actually confirmed whether he did indeed don a light beard or not.

Masa, though, noted immediately that when they met every morning, his new mentor was entirely clean-shaven. Of course, around noon a sparse and wiry growth would sprout and the *oni* would need to shave again. Oyaji, in fact, shaved three times a day, clipped his nails twice a day, and brushed his teeth before and after every meal. Masa was finally able to learn some manners.

He couldn't believe his luck.

One day Oyaji explained its reason for approaching him. It said that it was time to move on. Change its name, change its face, and change its town. For as small as Japan was, it was still a very big country for one lone creature; and besides, getting on in age, it felt the winters were too harsh. Oyaji then went on about how despite what was said about *oni*, some did prefer milder climates.

The *oni*'s dream was to live in the south, gaze over neatly trimmed tea bushes lining the hills and pilfer fat strawberries from the fields near the sea. But first, before it left, it needed to leave behind a disciple, someone to take over the art. Oyaji used a plate-sized hand behind Masa's head to turn the young man and pull him close, looking him dead in the eyes. Masa considered suggesting an extra daily brushing but correctly judged the timing not right.

"Your luck is about to change, little man." Oyaji laughed an enormous belly laugh that so filled the space around them that

Masa felt wholly safe. He, too, chuckled at his change of fortune and was soon howling and imitating his teacher by throwing his head back and slapping his sides.

But first there was training to do. Masa learned that there was still a generation who distrusted banks and kept their entire savings in the bottom of their chest of drawers. These people were very old now, usually living alone in Japanese-style houses with paper doors and tatami-matted floors. He was told that one of the reasons they lived so long was because they were always busy outside, working their little farms, playing ground golf with their friends or gossiping over the *daikons* at the vegetable market. The point being, they weren't always home.

Next, Masa practiced his speed and precision on the suitcase full of locks that Oyaji carried around. He learned how to invisibly eye a house for no less than one month before a job, how to resist the urge to remove his shoes when entering people's homes, and how to open drawers from the bottom up so he didn't have to worry about shutting them. Mostly he was taught to be *jimi*— not to stand out. While it was easier to pocket an entire stack of ten thousand yen bills and delight in the uproar it caused in the paper and on the news, it was much more prudent and wise to peel off one or two notes and let the suspicion fall on the miscalculation of an aging mind.

His final lesson, though, came at the end of three months, most unexpectedly in an *izakaya* after too many drinks.

"You'll go on your first job tomorrow," Oyaji said.

"What?" Masa half choked on the hot boiled tofu he had just spooned into his mouth. *But I'm not ready*, he thought.

"Old Mrs. Sano's place. We've been watching her long enough."

"Thank you!" The young man quickly adjusted his legs so that he was kneeling in the polite *seiza* position, straightened his back, and then bowed so low that his forehead rested on the floor for a long moment. Pushing himself up, he thought it odd that the old *oni* was not smiling. Instead, it looked sad.

"Also," Oyaji continued. "I'm leaving tonight."

"No." Masa's mouth continued to move, but he could think of nothing else to say. Oyaji loathed emotion. He believed it was what caused all man's problems. Masa wanted to prove that he had learned something during their time together, that he was ready to carry on the Five O'Clock Shadow's notorious name.

"Yes, on the last *kudari* train. Everything is settled here."

Masa always assumed his first job would be performed with his mentor, and that occasion was months, maybe years, away. But he knew there was no changing the creature's mind. He knew this was it.

Oyaji filled Masa's cup from the tall dark bottle of sake.

"By leaving I am handing the town over to you. I am showing that I trust you completely." He filled his own cup, shooing away Masa's attempt to do it for him. "As of this moment, I retire from my life of petty crime." He held up his glass, tilted it towards the young man once and downed the contents in one gulp. Masa did the same.

The rest of the night was spent in near silence. Masa listened to the scant last words of advice Oyaji imparted, finishing every drink poured for him, while obediently refilling the old *oni*'s glass as soon as it was set down.

In the end he was unable to see Oyaji off at the train station. All he had was the vague memory of a sloppy hug before he was pushed rather forcefully into a taxi and driven home.

≈

Masa overslept. It was 10:35. Old Mrs. Sano left for her Tuesday morning ground golf game at 9:00. Afterwards, she'd buy an *obento* with her lady friends and they'd eat lunch in the park. She'd return home at 1:30 for her afternoon nap. Masa checked the door. *Locked*, he thought. *But it's okay. I still have time.* The front *genkan* was one of those old-fashioned sliding doors—etched glass in an aluminum frame. It faced south. Being late August the old woman had hung a bamboo lattice blind to cut down on the heat. Masa thanked her for her kindness. It also provided protection from the occasional passerby.

The young man closed his eyes and took a deep breath. Pain,

remnants of the night before, cracked dry in his head. Oyaji had taught him to use all his senses, but to trust his eyes least of all. He explained that too much attention, importance, was placed on sight. The *oni* called it the seed of every mistake. Masa just now understood the second meaning to this statement; his teacher had probably received a lot of hassle in his life over his appearance. *Of course, you can't believe everything you see.*

Masa tried to smell the oil of the lock but only got a vague fishy odor from the bonito smoking plant down the road. His wrist was loose, bouncing, pressure, his concentration on the tip of the pick. He was trying hard to listen to the gentle rattle of the set pins, but instead heard only the deafening saw of cicadas in Old Mrs. Sano's dogwood tree.

Opening his eyes he squinted at his watch. He had been teasing the lock for almost five minutes. Oyaji demanded a time of forty-five seconds. There was, like a premonition, a vile lurch in his belly. This wasn't good.

Just then the door flew open and he fell forward with a grunt. There in front of him stood Old Mrs. Sano. She was wearing an apron, a bamboo racket-shaped futon-beater raised high over her head.

"Dorobo!" she screamed and began swinging in sharp downward chops. Masa curled into a fetal position, praying for the strength to stand up and run. *Whack! Whack! Whack!* She stepped down from the main house and into her slippers continuing her assault.

Suddenly she paused. "Officer!"

"Having some trouble here?"

Masa, beaten into the corner of the entryway loosened the grip on his head.

"I caught him!" The old woman was now poking Masa hard in the ribs with the stick end of the futon-beater. The young man flinched. There was no mistaking the joy in her voice.

"I caught The Five O'Clock Shadow!"

"Yes, you did. Good thing I was on patrol, too."

"And good thing you asked me to make those sweet dumplings for you today. Otherwise, I wouldn't have even been home."

Before he knew it, Masa was being pulled up like a naughty

cat, a strong pinch on the back of his neck. There he dangled—eyes screwed shut—in front of the policeman he was so afraid to see. *It can't be.* But Masa knew from the voice. It was him. He slowly opened his eyes.

"Oyaji." Masa's voice was weak, pleading.

"You hear that Mrs. Sano? This fellow thinks I'm his father." The officer gave him a hard look.

"I guess I must have knocked him too hard on the head." Mrs. Sano hid her weapon behind her back. "Whomped all the sense out of him."

"No, I think there's just something wrong with his eyes." The giant *oni* dressed in a pressed blue police uniform shook the trembling man gently. It smiled its usual forced smile, but the meaning was different.

"You are obviously mistaken, little man," it said and then began to laugh—a huge, booming laugh. *Not unlike hard kicks on a giant* taiko *drum or in the stomach*, Masa thought.

"I did a good job, huh?" the old woman asked, bouncing up and down on the balls of her feet.

"Yes, you did. I don't know what the department would do without you, Mrs. Sano."

The young man couldn't bear to look into the old *oni*'s amber-colored eyes. He turned his head and took a deep breath. The cologne hadn't changed. *Damn, he smelled good.* Masa, realizing there was no longer any need to perform for his mentor now, relaxed a little in the creature's grip and wept openly.

My devil's gate

"You're not going to put a toilet on your devil's gate!" Naomi's mother-in-law said, thumping the blueprints with her index finger.

"Excuse me?"

"Your devil's gate. Are you trying to destroy us all?"

It was all about rules and riddles and how many she didn't know. Naomi was born in Japan but soon moved to the States when her father's company opened a branch office in Chicago. She spent her entire life traveling back and forth and while she could speak Japanese fluently, there were all these cultural nuances she had never completely grasped. This was a fact she felt even more deeply since marrying her longtime boyfriend—a Japanese man who had been studying computer science at her university—and then moving back to his hometown.

There were two reasons that led Naomi to leave her family and friends and relocate to a small town halfway around the world. The first was her art. As a small child her mother introduced her to Japanese calligraphy. She taught Naomi how to lay out the *hanshi* rice paper, placing a felt pad underneath and two heavy, lacquered weights on each of the top corners. She learned the slow technique of rubbing ornate ink sticks against the *suzuri* stone while adding water drop by drop until a glossy black liquid pooled. Matters of posture, finger placement, and breath were also a part of the lessons. Naomi loved the craft and practiced daily, soon becoming so skilled she could no longer find anyone in the entire city to teach her. In her new home she was excited to search out an accomplished sensei and further her art.

Her second reason wasn't quite so obvious. Naomi loved her schools, her friends, and the neighborhoods she had grown up in. But whatever she did, wherever she was, there always lingered the shadow of displacement. Naomi felt different. And so even as a small girl she dreamed of one day locating that familiar place where she did fit in, where she felt entirely at ease. Coming to Japan for longer than a semester here or a semester there was her attempt to find her home.

Matters of chopsticks and bowing, slipper etiquette and gift giving were all relatively easy to embrace. Quirky differences that didn't hamper her daily life were almost second nature and in no way forced her to reevaluate her most basic ways of thinking.

For the first two months as a new bride in Japan she was sure she was right. But then came the day three elderly neighborhood women appeared at her door wringing their hands. It took two pots of green tea, an entire bag of rice crackers, and half the afternoon before the one that acted as their leader finally revealed the purpose of their visit.

"Naomi-chan," the leader woman said, cradling the tiny teacup in both hands. "We know it's difficult for a new wife. Money is tight. You're very busy."

"Not really, but—"

"We just want you to know, if we can be of any help," the old woman continued. "We're all on our pension, but we're awfully good with a needle and thread."

"Or we could put together a little money," a second woman chimed in.

"I'm afraid I don't understand," Naomi said.

"Those jeans you hang out on the line," the leader woman said. "They are an embarrassment."

"Embarrassment?"

"The ones, with the holes in the knees," said woman number two.

"Shameful," piped in the third woman who immediately averted her eyes and resumed nibbling her cracker.

"People walk by and see those and think—" The leader woman rested her warm hand on Naomi's forearm.

"Poverty," it was the third woman again. "They think you don't have enough money to afford decent clothes." She was readying herself to leave. The message had been delivered.

And then there was the time Naomi purchased a new refrigerator for their house. This faux pas would have gone undiscovered if her mother-in-law had not been over that day dropping off some *daikon* radishes she had grown in her garden when the deliverymen arrived.

"Who could that be?" her mother-in-law asked when the doorbell rang.

"Oh, it's probably the new refrigerator. You should see it. I got a great deal," Naomi said, thinking her husband's penurious mother would be thrilled and beg to hear details.

"You didn't have them deliver it today!"

"Yes, today's the earliest they could bring it," Naomi said.

"Today's is—" Naomi's mother-in-law hurried to consult the wall calendar, ran her finger over the dates, the tiny writing in the corner of each square. "Just as I thought, today's a *butsumetsu*. You can't have anything delivered today!"

That was the time the young wife received a three-hour lecture on *rokuyo*—the belief that every single day of the year is one of six varieties, each with varying degrees of luckiness and unluckiness. Naomi listened politely to how only fools and the impoverished began any day without first a close inspection of the calendar. Important events such as weddings, funerals, and home deliveries required even more caution.

Nevertheless, not all matters concerned complete neighborhood disgrace or ill-fated appliances. There was the evening that Naomi and her husband spent with her in-laws eating tasty dishes of grilled eel and rice. Conversation and moods were light and interesting right up until the moment Naomi plucked a pickled plum from the jar that always sat at the end of the table and dropped it into her bowl.

"Well, I'm not going to rush you to the emergency room," her mother-in-law said.

"Excuse me?"

"The pickled plum," Naomi's husband explained. "There is some superstition that says you're not supposed to eat them with eel. It messes up your stomach. I wouldn't worry too much about it."

"I see," Naomi said, wondering which would be a greater sin, returning it to the jar or throwing it away.

"You haven't heard what happened to my big sister, then," Naomi's mother-in-law began.

Judging from the exaggerated degree her husband and father-in-law rolled their eyes, Naomi imagined they had heard this one before.

"If you come over tomorrow I'll write out a list of foods that should not be eaten together. You can study it and we'll avoid any mishaps in the future."

The vague disquiet within Naomi returned—and this time much worse, maybe because she had so much faith in Japan being the place where she fit in. For a while she hung her laundry indoors until she began to worry that the elderly women in the neighborhood would suspect her ill and unable to perform household duties; that at any moment they might again gather forces and show up on her doorstep to chat.

From nowhere could she muster the strength to attend the family dinners she had at one time enjoyed so much. She stayed inside, occasionally practiced her calligraphy, and took long afternoon naps. At night she retired early and in the morning couldn't wake up without hitting the snooze button once or twice.

Her husband grew concerned about her, asked what he could do to help. But Naomi insisted she was fine, just a little blue. It would run its course in time. Her husband brought home flowers and took her on long drives. They discussed starting a family but thought the house they were renting much too small for that.

A month or so later her husband came home with news. He'd been secretly researching, talking to some people, and had decided that they were financially able to move, to build their own house. He'd even found a piece of land for sale in a newer neighborhood, one with younger families that were sure not to uphold all the old traditions so rigidly. It would be a new start.

Slowly Naomi brightened. Flipping through magazines and sketching out designs of their new home gave her a thrill. She became close to the contractor and he was receptive to her ideas, even encouraged them. He boasted that once they had finished building there would be an open house and visitors were sure to be inspired by her design. He thanked her in advance for the customers it would bring.

Her mind engrossed in debates of carpet or tatami, paint or wallpaper, Naomi was aware of her depression lifting. When they announced the day construction would begin, she hesitantly checked the calendar and was relieved to see the day fell on a *taian*, Great Peace, a day good for just about everything. She felt so confidant that she called her in-laws and invited them over for dinner. Naomi prepared a meal of breaded pork cutlets, shredded cabbage, and miso soup. She couldn't wait to show her mother-in-law the blueprints for the house. After dinner she spread them across the floor and invited everyone over to look.

"You're not going to put a toilet on your devil's gate!" her mother-in-law said.

"Excuse me?"

"Your devil's gate. Do you want to destroy us all? It's the northeastern direction. That is your *kimon*, your devil's gate. You must never, ever put a toilet there. No water, fire, windows or doors, and especially nothing dirty like a toilet." Naomi's mother-in-law shook her head in disbelief. She retrieved a magnifying glass from her purse and examined the plans more thoroughly.

"And these stairs," she said, indicating the middle of the paper. "Your luck is going to walk in the front door, shoot up those stairs and exit this back window here." The old woman turned to address her son. "And why didn't you tell her about any of this?"

Naomi settled in beside her mother-in-law casting a yes, why-didn't-you-tell-me-anything-about-this glare at her husband before trying to decipher what exactly a devil's gate was.

"I just thought those were old superstitions," he said. "The realtor didn't seem to mention them."

"Those jackals are only out for money," she said. "They'd build on your great grandfather's grave if you gave them enough persuasion."

"Oh." Naomi's husband grimaced an *I'm sorry* in her direction.

"*Kaso,*" her mother-in-law began, "is a kind of physiognomy of a house. And by house I mean, school, office, temple, any building at all. Everything affects *kaso*—the movement of the earth, light, heat, wind, and especially the flow of *ki*."

Naomi knew about *ki*—the invisible energy force that permeates every living thing—from all her years of watching old karate and kung fu flicks.

Her mother-in-law went into some of the complex rules that needed to be observed when buying, renting, or building a house. How there are auspicious directions to place front doors, living rooms, bedrooms, and stairs. And how on the other hand, there are directions that bring sickness, poverty, or a son that won't study for his finals.

Most likely sensing the doubt that Naomi felt, she began a story about a family friend whose husband received a raise. It was such a wonderful raise that they were able to move from their apartment into a new house. Within weeks of the move her husband's company went bankrupt. He searched for another job with no luck. Finally, they hired a professional to come in and look at their *kaso*. He found several things wrong but was able to correct them without too much trouble. A week later the husband obtained his lifelong dream of working in the shaved fish business making even more money than at his previous company. They'd been happy ever since.

"But why?" Naomi asked, slightly curious about the origins. "Why devil's gate?"

Her father-in-law said he'd heard of a Chinese legend that told of a large army of devils invading from the northeast thus starting the belief in the unlucky direction.

Her husband laughed and said, no, in fact he had read that the coldest winds blow from the northeast and that's the reason windows and doors are avoided. That's also why it's often suggested that you plant a tree there, not to keep out the devils but to block the freezing winter gusts.

"Yes, those both make sense. But what do they have to do with a toilet?" Naomi asked.

Her mother-in-law chuckled at the men's explanations and began with her theory, which involved the movement of *ki* and how it's in the northeast direction that this *ki* changes from yin to yang and back again. That it's a turbulent and delicate area and should be quiet and calm. A closet is always a good thing to put there, she said. She also asserted that having something filthy there like a toilet would draw dirty and negative *ki* throughout the house. And bad *ki* is the cause of sickness, money troubles, and a host of other atrocious things.

The old woman then retrieved a ruler, a pencil, and a compass from a drawer. She measured to find the center of the house, drew a straight line through that point stretching from magnetic north to south, again from east to west and lastly bisected those with lines that ran from southwest to northeast. This last line is the *kimon sen*, devil's gate line she pointed out. While it's best not to put any of the offenders 15 degrees on either side of the line, at the very least there shouldn't be any one of the taboos on the line itself.

"But it can't be fixed. They're building the house now," Naomi said, looking to her husband and father-in-law for help. "They're almost finished."

"It's okay," her mother-in-law said. "I know what we can do. I know how we can fix this."

A week later found Naomi and her mother-in-law kneeling on the floor of a leaning, nearly decrepit temple waiting for someone called simply the Knower to appear. The room smelled of mildewed wood and old incense smoke. Above their heads water stains ringed the once-expensive cedar ceiling, in places seeping discoloration down sand-covered walls. Directly in front of them, seemingly out of place, rose an elaborate shrine gilded in red and gold, and in the middle of that, towering above everything else, stood a porcelain statue of the female Buddha *Kannon*. It was surrounded by dozens of vases full of tall stargazer lilies or yellow chrysanthemums, blooms as big around as a child's face.

This might have been like any other shrine Naomi had observed in Japan except that on almost every available surface there were taped photographs of people: old men lying in hospital beds, middle-aged women looking up from meals of noodles, and teenage girls posing for the camera. There were even photos of small children caught in some act of play, infants swaddled in soft-looking blankets. The affect was quite disturbing.

"The Knower knows," Naomi's mother-in-law spoke quietly. "She knows things no one else does. And she has the power to make things right. I had to pull a lot of strings to get a meeting with her. She can help us, I'm sure." And then, noticing her daughter-in-law staring at the photographs, she added, "Those are the people she is praying for now."

"You mean they are all sick?" Naomi asked.

"Sick or having some sort of trouble—money, finances, grades."

Naomi's stomach gave a squeamish turn, but she didn't have time to consider it as at the same moment an elderly woman slipped out from behind a curtain and made her way across the floor.

"There she is," Naomi's mother-in-law whispered.

The Knower appeared to be blind. She wore dark glasses and walked with hesitant steps but no cane. She took the corner around the shrine too fast and bumped into a wooden stand holding a bowl-shaped bell, nearly knocking it over.

"Welcome," the Knower said, holding both arms out. Stopping a good two meters from where Naomi and her mother-in-law were seated, she faced the open expanse of the room and continued.

"I'm so glad the four of you could visit me today," the Knower said.

Naomi squinted her eyes at her mother-in-law and mouthed *four?* She was promptly ignored.

"Thank you for having us," said Naomi's mother-in-law. "I know you're so terribly busy." The Knower nonchalantly adjusted her position on the floor and scooted on her knees so that she was sitting closer to the two.

The blind woman then reached out, first patting Naomi's mother-in-law on the knee before finding the young wife. When the Knower did fumble upon Naomi's forearm she recoiled quickly pulling both hands to her chest.

"Something terrible is going to happen," the Knower said. "Something awful." She rubbed the fingers that had brushed Naomi as if they'd been burned.

"I know, I know," said Naomi's mother-in-law. "That is why we are here."

Naomi's mother-in-law began in detail about the devil's gate fiasco. The blueprints were again rolled out across the floor, four candle holders acting as paper weights. Despite the burden of being completely sightless, the Knower removed a compass from her pocket and placed it on the paper. She pushed it around making a clucking sound in the back of her throat and saying, "I see, I see."

It took fifteen minutes of discussion until it was decided that a series of talismans would be created and imbued with prayers of protection. This would take several months, the Knower informed, payment would be welcome once they were completed. The simple act of hanging the assigned ornament in the proper place would restore the house's *ki* to its correct balance and all would be well. A year later new ones could be purchased for a ten percent discount.

Before they left Naomi's mother-in-law withdrew an envelope from her apron pocket and slid it across the floor.

"Thank you for today," she said, bowing low. Naomi couldn't help but notice how thick the envelope was. Using her sensitive fingertips, the Knower located the gift and accepted it graciously. When she turned to place it on the shrine at the feet of *Kannon*, she knocked over an incense burner full of ash causing them all to sneeze.

≈

Naomi and her husband tried not to laugh as she retold the story of her visit with the Knower, how the elderly woman thought there were four people there, how until she heard their voices she sat halfway across the room, and how when making her exit she missed the curtain-veiled door and walked straight into the wall. Naomi didn't mention the woman's prediction of something terrible happening.

"Well, I can't say she instills much trust in me," he said.

"Me either," Naomi answered. "What should we do? We did kind of ask her to make the good luck charms. I guess it would be rude to tell her we've changed our minds."

"I suppose you're right. Do they match the colors of the rooms?" Naomi's husband joked.

"Now, that's a good question," Naomi said.

≈

Two months later Naomi and her husband spent their first night in their new house. Naomi slept better than she had in months. She noted no bad vibes or cold winds, not so much as a single devil's mischievous prank. Everything was perfect.

Nonetheless, the next day her in-laws arrived with a handful of talismans and a platter full of take-out sushi. Naomi examined each charm, admiring the gorgeous characters brushed down the colorful boards.

"Did she write these herself?" Naomi asked.

"Of course, she's quite an accomplished calligrapher," her mother-in-law said.

"Who would have guessed?" Naomi lifted her eyebrows at her husband. "I wonder if she takes on students."

Eating was postponed until all the charms were hung in their appropriate places and a quick prayer offered to boost the effect. It was as if their luck was already changing for the better, each talisman matched the color scheme of the room it was hung in perfectly.

They all sat down to dinner amidst the still-unpacked boxes that lined the walls.

"We wanted to tell you our good news," Naomi announced. "We're going to have a baby." Naomi reached over and squeezed her husband's hand.

"That's wonderful," her mother-in-law said, smiling.

"It gets better than that," Naomi's husband hinted.

"Yes, we're going to have twins," Naomi said.

"How far along are you?" her mother-in-law asked.

"Three months."

"I knew it. That means you were pregnant when we went to see the Knower," her mother-in-law said.

"Yes, I guess so," Naomi said.

There was a moment when everyone exchanged a glance, a moment before it sunk in.

"'The four of you,'" Naomi remembered. "The Knower said, 'So glad the *four* of you could make it.'"

"That's creepy," her husband said.

"That's the Knower. She knew," Naomi's mother-in-law stated, grinning from ear to ear. "The Knower is never wrong. Never."

≈

Morning sickness temporarily leaving her queasy to the smell of calligraphy ink, Naomi explored a new hobby. She began to research all the various superstitions and old sayings that she was confronted with almost daily.

She spent some time and actually learned the list of incompatible foods, going as far as to find out the various reasons given for the stories. She found that one of the theories behind the pickled plum/eel mystery was simply that pickled plum is thought to increase a person's appetite. And if there is one thing you do not want when serving expensive eel it's a person with an insatiable appetite.

The more she studied, the more the folk legends intrigued her. Nothing was as simple as it seemed on the surface. There were layers under layers, each needing to be peeled back and examined. Naomi even started a notebook that she filled with her favorite superstitions and old wives' tales.

≈

One day five years later Naomi and her husband took their boys on a little hike in the hills near their home. When they reached a grassy plateau she spread out a blanket and unpacked the *obento* boxed lunches she had fixed earlier that morning.

She watched the boys scamper off with their father to play for a bit when she was suddenly overwhelmed with how utterly happy she was with her life. Naomi might never fit entirely into either culture, but she accepted that. She had found her place with her husband and the boys. However, recently when that euphoria welled up inside her so did a new needling in the back of her thoughts. A feeling that things were too good.

"Look! Look!" her eldest called.

"It's huge," said her second son.

Naomi hurried over to see what the fuss was about. Her husband and the two boys formed a semicircle, all three of them pointing to the ground. There on the path a fat earthworm was slowly working its way across the dirt.

"Pretty impressive, huh?" her husband added.

"Just so you know," Naomi warned. "You guys had better not pee on it."

"Eyuu," the boys sang in unison.

"What are you talking about?" Naomi's husband asked, looking at her like she was insane.

"I've read about this. If you pee on a worm your private parts will burn," she said.

The boys giggled, stepped over the oblivious bug, and trotted back to the blanket and their lunches. Naomi looked on as they opened their *obento* boxes and simultaneously plucked out the octopus-shaped sausages with their fingers. Her heart swelled with emotion before panic seized it. In her head she could hear clearly her mother-in-law's voice, *the Knower is never wrong. Never.* The blind woman had been right about the twins, but what about the other thing? That something awful would happen. From the day it happened Naomi knew in her gut that the Knower had not been referring to the devil's gate or the misplacement of some stairs. Naomi knew that something was coming.

"Hurry up, before we eat it all," her husband called from the blanket.

"I'm coming," Naomi said. Walking over, she wondered about the lives of all the people staring out from those pictures taped to the Knower's shrine. She wondered if every one of them was okay now. "Hey, before we eat, let's take a family picture," she said, retrieving the camera from her bag.

ganguro and the mountain witch

BEST FRIENDS

"Hold still!" Mariko was applying a fat stroke of kohl eyeliner to Hina's eyes. "The dark goes on the inside, the thicker the better. See, I use my little finger as a guide." The girl held up her pinky to her own face and indeed the black outline was at least the same width as her finger. "Don't move."

"It's not me," Hina insisted, bracing her Doc Martins on the scuffed linoleum floor while trying to ignore the stares of the other passengers riding the late afternoon train. *What a way to spend my sixteenth birthday*, Hina thought.

"Next I'll paint white all around that, up to your eyebrows— which we'll need to shave off if we're going to do this properly —and down both sides of your nose." Hina cringed at the coldness of the makeup. She could feel its pastiness clump in the fine hair on her face. "If you want I can take care of these eyebrows now. I have a straight razor in here somewhere." Just then the train leaned into a turn causing Mariko to lose her balance and stumble.

"No, no, that's okay," Hina answered.

There was a short hiss of a speaker being turned on followed by the nasal-voiced conductor announcing the next stop. A half-dozen passengers gathered their belongings and shuffled their way to the doors. Only after securing themselves to the dangling plastic rings overhead did each gaze return one by one to the two teenage girls.

"And this is called what now?" Hina asked. Once inseparable, Hina and Mari had grown apart the past year. Ever since Mari stormed out of third-period history class declaring that no old, dead people could teach her anything, Hina hardly saw her childhood best friend. These days they communicated almost entirely by text messages on their cell phones.

"*Ganguro.*" Mariko briefly stopped her work while the train switched tracks and listed hard to the right before it slowed.

"Blackened face?"

"That or *gan gan guro*, you know, really, really black. I haven't figured out which one it is. But it's all the rage in Shibuya and Ikebukuro."

"So girls then willingly do this?" Hina's shock still hadn't worn off since seeing her best friend show up after school with her hair sprayed cotton-candy pink, her face painted dark brown and highlighted with bold black lines, white eyelids and lips and a gooey-looking web of false eyelashes. The train screeched to a stop and the doors opened. A group of high school boys pushed onto the train, laughing as they tried yanking down each other's hip-hugging slacks. They didn't immediately notice the two girls taking up an entire bench to themselves. Hina recognized the disheveled uniforms and wide necks. They were judo players from West High School. *No one I know, thank goodness.*

"So this is going to make us popular?" Hina whispered.

"It's going to make you popular, girlie. I'm already way ahead of my time." Mariko posed by pursing her white lips and batting her sticky-looking mass of lashes.

"Mm-hm," Hina said. "That's what they all said in school when you quit last year."

"What?"

"Nothing."

"Damn right." Mariko stayed focused on her task, now applying a series of rainbow-colored gemstones to her friend's cheek with tweezers and glue. "You know what we really need to do? Get you to a tanning salon. Or a beach."

"Oh yeah?"

"For now I just used this extra dark base coat. But until you get *gan gan* black all over, it's going to look a bit silly. White from the shoulders down, you know?"

"Mmm." Hina wasn't really paying attention. Instead, she was observing one of the judo player's profiles. *He must be new to the team*, she thought. He didn't have that mauled look about him, his hair was still longish, and the line of his nose was completely in tact. Hina inhaled. Even from where she sat she caught a waft of Abercrombie & Fitch's Fierce. Somehow she knew he was the source.

"These country bumpkins won't know what hit them," Mariko said, removing a hibiscus flower from her pocket and pinning it into Hina's hair. "There!"

"So how do I look?" Hina asked, trying not to fidget when she noticed that the boys had quieted down and were stealing curious glances in their direction.

"Here, take a look." Mariko retrieved a hand mirror from her bag. Hina squealed.

"Hey, look!" The boy with the ears that resembled two enormous pot stickers was pointing their way and addressing his buddies. "I'm scared. We've got a couple of *yamamba* on the train."

"Mountain witches?" Hina pressed the mirror to her face and began combing her bangs down over it with her fingers.

"Yeah, it's just another name for *gan guro*," Mariko said, rolling the top of her short skirt up. Once she received a chorus of hoots and whistles from the boys she blew a kiss over her shoulder and plopped down on the seat next to Hina. "That'll shut them up for a while."

"Do you know I have to listen to *yamamba* gossip nightly from everyone down at Ochoko?" Hina said from behind the hand mirror. "There's a rumor that there's one living in the mountains by our house."

"Girl, you DO live in the sticks. People still believe in that stuff?"

"Not only that, but every night someone has a new story. In the past month we've lost three stray cats, one dog, and Old Mr. Oda woke from a nap to find his garden destroyed and all the fish he had drying in the sun vanished." Hina dropped the mirror to her lap. The slathered-on makeup that covered her face left an eerie dark and white impression on the mirror, an impression she tried nervously to erase with her thumb. "Oh, and last week Taneishi-san was bathing in one of those hot springs up in the hills when he swore the mountain witch snuck up on him and stole his clothes. He said she chased him buck-naked all the way to the vegetable market. He's got a cold to prove it."

"Fools," Mariko said.

"I know. It's insane. But you can't tell them anything. I really need to get out of this hole."

"You know, if you're not careful you're going to end up just like your mother."

Hina was silent. When she woke up that morning she felt entirely different than she had every other day of her life. She followed her normal routine: threw yesterday's laundry in the washing machine, made her own lunch, washed the dishes, and headed out to school. But always there was a constant nagging in the back of her brain, a desperate voice—a screaming almost—that she couldn't quite make out. Even her body felt different. Inside her chest moved something massive and ill at ease. For some reason, Hina was both terrified and hyperaware at the same time. One week ago a remark like "you're going to end up just like your mother" would have incited a bout of playful fighting; today it brought nothing because there was something bigger going on.

Receiving no reaction, Mariko threw herself back against the cushioned seat and stretched her long legs. "So what do you have planned for tonight? Ochoko? Wanna do something after?"

"I don't know. I might need to meet Tai-chan."

"So you're still seeing Noodle-boy, huh?" Mariko smoothed her miniskirt and scanned it for lint.

"Don't call him that."

"I don't care how cute he is. His father owns a ramen shop and he's in line to get it next. You're going to be eating noodles every day for the rest of your life. Do you know how fat you're going to get? Hence, my previous prediction."

"Oh, stop it."

"I guess it wouldn't be so bad if you guys were doing it."

"Mari!" Hina threatened, glancing at the high school boys to see if they had overheard.

"It's true, though. You are a prude," Mariko said. "You're poor and you're a prude. There is nothing worse than a self-righteous poor person."

"Well, you're a . . ."

Before Hina could finish, Mariko's cell phone began to ring the theme to *The Godfather*. Sliding it open, Mariko stuck her tongue out at Hina and answered it with a lispy baby-voice, "*Moshi moshi.*"

Hina rolled her eyes and busied herself replacing the hand mirror into her best friend's duffel bag. It was then that she noticed the Fendi purse and a pair of Louis Vuitton thigh-high leather boots stuffed in among several changes of clothes still in the dry cleaner's plastic. Pretty sure of what she'd find, Hina checked the label of what looked like a salmon-colored halter dress. Chanel.

Mariko cooed and tittered into the phone. Wrapping a long, stiff strand of pink hair around her finger she giggled a time, repeated a place, and slid the phone shut.

"Where did you get all this?" Hina asked.

"I got a job." Mariko used the clunky heel of one of her Lucite platform shoes to gently kick Hina out of her bag. "If you had one, you'd have nice stuff, too."

"I have a job," Hina said.

"That's right, helping your mommy work in that dive of a bar. I'm sure you're making a fortune."

"As I recall you used to want to work there."

"Not anymore. I'm making real money now," Mariko said. "Another year or two and I'll have enough to travel."

"Yeah, right."

"What are your dreams?" Mariko asked.

"Dreams?"

"I know you want to go to college. Do you really think your mama-san is going to pay for you to run off after high school?"

Hina shrugged.

"Heck, you're half the reason those old men stumble into that bar. If you leave then big mama doesn't eat."

"You're so mean."

"No, I'm serious. And that sister of yours. What's up with her? She wants out of there just as bad as you do. First man she snags"—Mariko made a jerking motion with her thumb—"she's history."

"Probably," Hina said.

"And if you go and tell me that you think you're going to marry ramen boy and he'll save you, then you're not as smart as I thought you were."

With Mariko absent Hina hadn't confided her worries to anyone. It was unnerving how Mari still managed to hit on them one after another. *If only she had a little more tact*, Hina thought. It made that itchiness in her blood flair again.

"Okay, then, what's the answer?" Hina asked.

"This." Mariko dug through her duffel bag and removed her bankbook. Turning it to the last page she passed it to her friend.

"I don't believe it!" Hina said.

"Have you ever seen so many zeros?" Mariko laughed.

"But how did you . . ."

Mariko tapped her cell phone. "With this."

"Who did you just talk to? It sounded like plans for a date." Hina was starting to catch on.

"It was, sort of." Mariko held up eight fingers. "Eighty thousand yen for one date."

"You're insane."

"I've actually got my own regulars but they have friends. I'm looking to make some introductions. You'd be perfect."

"You can't be serious." Hina felt breathless.

"They're teachers, most of them, a few office workers. Nice guys, if you can get past the bald heads and fish-belly paunches. I'd let you choose, and I'd help you weed out the creeps and the perverts. I'm good at spotting them."

"You're disgusting."

"Am I? A little sacrifice now and I'll be set for later. I prefer to call it investing in my future, making the best of what choices are given to me. You see, I believe I can change my life."

Hina crossed her arms in front of her chest and turned her head away from her friend.

"I'm thinking a year or two and then I'm going to travel around the world—Australia, England, America." Mariko snatched the bankbook from her friend, curled it in one hand above her head and assumed the classic Statue of Liberty pose. "And look good while doing it. Who knows? I may just meet some local and set-tle down." She put her arms behind her head and closed her eyes. "Big house in the country, an outdoor pool, a garage to park my minivan, two dogs, two cats, and a half a dozen kids each with his own room, and a hottie husband who adores me." Mariko sighed. "It's not even as bad as you think it is."

"Isn't it?"

"Fine, fine. I was just trying to help." Mariko moved away. "Besides, you have a prince charming."

The train slowed into another station and most of the pas-sengers got off.

"Do you know how much ramen sellers make?" Mariko asked. Hina didn't answer so Mariko tried a different tactic. "If you're so in love with this noodle guy then marry him. But before that why not make yourself a little nest egg so you two don't have to live with his parents above that reeking restaurant for the rest of your lives. Or, hey, why not use some of the money to get that mother of yours out of debt? Buy her the bar, your filial piety is done, and you can move out."

"Oh, Mari," was all Hina could say.

"Think about it." Mariko stood and shouldered her bag. Before zipping it shut, she pulled out a small package wrapped in yellow paper and ribbons. "You didn't think I'd forget, did you?" She placed the box in Hina's lap.

"Thanks," Hina said pulling it close to her stomach.

"Listen, call me or text me tonight if you change your mind. We can go on a double-date. You don't even have to do anything. We'll have a little birthday party for you. My gosh, woman, you're

sixteen now. We need to celebrate. No business, I promise."
Mariko stepped out onto the platform and then turned to yell.
"My treat!"

MAMA-SAN

Hina walked home through the park, swinging her unopened
present in one hand. Feeling the heavy thunk of its insides shifting back and forth, she wondered what it was. Hina lived with
her mother and sister at the end of a dilapidated row of pre-
war mom-and-pop shops. Back then, the story went, the street
was one big family, a hodgepodge of goods and services where
everyone sold something someone else needed.

There were rice venders, cloth dyers, and wooden *geta*-shoe
menders. A man who spent all day pressing black ink into
embossed sticks and another who carved the stones needed
to grind them back into a shiny ebony-blue liquid. Calligraphy
brushes could be purchased right next door where a quiet woman
collected horse, goat, and badger hair all day long and then spent
her evenings weaving it carefully around lacquered lengths of
bamboo. She hung the finished products along the rafters where
they waited a summer breeze and the compliments of passersby.
Residents would gather in the shadow of her awning to discuss
the August heat and how the brushes clicking a song like hollow
wind chimes seemed to cool them off.

Nowadays, though, every store had settled into some variety
of bar—the weary, overly suspicious owners residing upstairs
uninterested in small talk, much less friendship.

There were colorful Filipino pubs with Polaroids of their host-
esses taped pyramid-style on the front windows. Nights when
customers were scant, the girls passed the time by eagerly decorating their photos with pastel-colored Milky pens—drawing
hearts and lip marks and signing names like Bunny and Rose.

The Japanese hostess bars, on the other hand, were solemn
with thick-velvet-curtained windows and only the occasional
spill of a drunk's forlorn karaoke wail to let you know they were
open. These places promised an entirely different kind of night.

Hina's mother's bar was the oldest, the only one existing through four generations, a simple *izakaya* with tatami mats and low tables, a short bar, and all the boiled fishcakes you could eat. Named simply after the tiny cup used to drink sake, it was called Ochoko. Although recently, men confusing the literal meaning of the word for the newer slang one occasionally slipped in under the parted curtains only to be shooed away by mother in a foul mood promising to salt and skewer some part of their anatomy.

"What the hell happened to you?" Standing on the top of an arched stone bridge was a woman so short and round that today Hina couldn't shake the unnerving feeling that if she accidentally bumped into her, the woman's skin might split like an overripe plum and spill cushy innards all over her feet. Hina raised a hand to her face remembering the train ride and Mariko's handiwork. "Did you get in a fight?"

"No," Hina said.

The city bells chimed 4:30, announcing the end of the work-day for the fishermen. Despite the late hour it was obvious this woman had just woken up. She wore faded blue sweats under a satin Hello Kitty robe. Her thinning black and purple hair had recently been combed smooth into large curlers and set into rows on her head. Hina cringed at how obvious yesterday's makeup clung dry in familiar lines and valleys across the woman's face. She knew that instead of washing it off, her mother would merely reapply a new coat in an hour or so and start another night.

"You'd better get home and clean up then," her mother said. "I'm not going to have you scaring away customers."

"That's a big one." Hina pointed to the cage that swung from a long chain ending in loops around her mother's wrist. Inside, a rat the size of a toy chihuahua paced back and forth. By pre-monition or instinct it suddenly decided that up was the safest direction and, gripping the rusted metals bars with its pink, long-clawed feet, it began to climb.

"Must be a mom. Look at that belly." Her mother pulled the cage up to eye level for Hina to see.

The girl gazed over her shoulder instead. From the other side of the park she spotted her older sister fussing with the strap of one of her high heels. *Another Friday night date*, Hina thought.

Kotone was a full sixteen years older than Hina and gorgeous. But she could not—no matter how hard she tried—keep a boyfriend for any length of time. Two years ago Kotone began meeting men via a local arranged-marriage service. Last month she went on her last date through them. There were no more single men left in town, they'd told her. Among bows and apologies for not trying hard enough, they presented her with a lovely toaster oven and said they'd send a postcard when someone new and available signed up. There was a lot of confusion around town as to why such a pretty girl could not get married, but Hina knew why.

"You look like shit." Kotone had caught up to them.

"Thank you," Hina said. "You're looking lovely yourself."

"Humph!"

Hina glanced back to the rat clinging to the top of the cage and felt a sudden jolt of pity for it. It maneuvered its way to face her.

"You two missed the excitement last night. Mori-san was in." Her mother lowered the cage and balanced it at her feet on the low lip of the bridge. She lit a cigarette, extinguishing the match with an exaggerated flick of her wrist.

"That dolt always comes in," Kotone said, snatching the pack from her mother's hand and removing a cigarette for herself.

"You noticed he was late though? Didn't make it in until after midnight." Hina's mother leaned over and blew smoke from her Lucky Strike into the cage. "Finished off half a bottle of Isojin sake, can you believe it? I haven't pushed a bottle of that in years. It seems his wife wandered off early yesterday morning and hasn't been seen since."

"That's awful," Hina said.

"So, what? He was out celebrating then last night?" Kotone said. "The best sake in town. I'm a bachelor again! Drinks on me!"

Mother laughed, shaking the cage at her feet unnecessarily.

"Distraught," she explained. "He waited until the search party was over for the night. Would you believe he wouldn't even go home until the sun came up? Scared witless."

"So it's true then," Kotone said. "About the *yamamba*?"

"Seems so," Mother said.

Hina held her tongue. She concentrated on the rat as it used its grip to push its twitching nose through the bars. The creature was staring at her, seemed to be trying to communicate something with its watery eyes. The gathering ache swelled in her chest again when she heard the animal whisper, *Run, run!*

"I need to get going," Kotone said. "You look like a clown that got hit by a bus, by the way." She pointed to Hina. *Always the last word.* "And what's this? Your girlfriend get you a present?" Kotone poked the box.

Hina expected her big sister to forget, but when she saw her mother laughing as well she looked once more at the rat and thought, the voice loud inside her, *Wanna trade places?*

Hina had tried to be friends with her older sister, and a couple of times even asked her to go with her to the mother/daughter conferences at school. It was embarrassing having a mother who worked nights and despised having to haul herself anywhere before noon and then to attempt to balance dangerously in the tiny chairs and hear how smart her youngest was. "If she's doing fine, why did I have to even show up?" she reprimanded a teacher once. Kotone always refused to go, though, and with even more vileness than was normal for her.

Hina's sister strutted off, tossing her cigarette butt into the river below.

"Don't mind her," Mother said, pointing to Kotone. "She's always been high strung."

"Yeah." When Hina turned back she watched her mother lowering the cage into the fast running water. Swinging it by the long chain, she was trying to find the deepest part of the river and missed. The cage caught on some rocks and fell sideways, half in and half out of the current. Hina wasn't sure, but over the rush of water she thought she heard the animal's squeals, its frantic scratching on the metal, and it screaming *run, run, escape before it's too late!*

"You're awful," Hina said to her amused mother.

Finally, with a yank of the chain the cage washed into a deep crevice. The white froth softly buried the rat and the screaming.

"I'm going home," Hina said.

The Mountain Witch

Hina washed her face and lay down for a nap. She woke up to her phone buzzing its way across the tatami floor. *Tai-chan*, she thought. He always called to wake her up before she went to work. Reaching to answer it, the girl felt something slide from her chest and hit the floor. *The electronic dictionary!* For as long as Hina could remember she had wanted one. Despite the crowd she hung out with, she really did love to crack a book. The girl picked it up, examined it for damages and remembered why Mariko was still her best friend.

"*Moshi, moshi*," Hina said into the phone.

"You awake?"

"Yeah."

"So is tonight going to be our special night?" Tai-chan asked.

Hina could hear the sound of water running and dishes clacking together in a sink. She had been trying to forget about the promise they'd made last year, the promise Tai-chan had been reminding her of for nearly five months.

"I don't know." She was in no mood to make a decision like this right now.

"It's your birthday. Come on," he said. She could tell he was walking away from the noise to a quieter part of the restaurant. "I've reserved us a room at the Let's-Come-Together Inn."

"I'll tell you what. If you get a call from me after work then it's a go. Otherwise . . ." Hina worried she'd have to defend her point, but their conversation was interrupted by the booming voice of Tai-chan's father.

"Okay, I gotta go. But really, think about it. I bought flowers"— he paused—"and stuff."

The regulars were all sitting cross-legged on the tatami floors by 7:30; by 9:00 they were full of skewered chicken yakitori, cold tofu with fish shavings, and grilled eggplant drizzled in miso sauce. Mori-san had come in early and remained planted on a stool at the bar drinking his sake from the corner of the *masu*. Mother, feeling pity for her old friend, placed the small cedar box—which she kept for special occasions—into a deep bowl and poured in the milk-cloudy sake until it overflowed, filling the dish as well as the box. She usually wouldn't allow so much drink to go unpaid for, but today Old Mori-san was hurting and mother always boasted that her heart was at least as big as her ass.

By midnight, everyone except Mr. Mori had returned home.

"Hina, are you going out?" Mother asked, raking some leftover fried rice into the middle of the rat trap and then using a slippered foot to nudge it into a corner.

"Yeah, I was thinking about grabbing a cup of coffee with Mari." This had always been the story. Every Friday and Saturday night no matter what all-night disco, karaoke box sing-a-thon, or fireworks-on-the-beach event was planned, Hina told her mother she was going to sit in a 24-hour café and sip coffee with Mariko, maybe do some studying as well.

"Listen, I need to clean up the kitchen. Can you walk Mori-san back home? He's the old house behind Octopus Park."

"Which old house?" Hina asked, remembering vaguely how her mother used to take her there to play when she was very small.

"There's only one now. It's kind of on the way, isn't it?"

"Sure," Hina answered, thinking that it wasn't on the way at all. Slumped over the bar, the drunken old man slept quietly on the now empty *masu*, the bowl balancing upside-down on his bald head. For the last two hours it had been refilled with hot water, but Mori-san was too stubborn and sad to notice and continued to get drunk anyway.

"Does that guy still live with him?" Hina asked, remembering the rumors about Mori-san's son. She had never seen the man herself, only heard the stories. Tales of a man who was so insane even the local hospital wouldn't take him. His parents kept him tied in a room and appeased him with manga and TV. If he missed even one episode of *Naruto*, they said he would chew through the ropes and escape the house looking for anyone to maim and eventually kill. They say he actually got a girl once. The things he did to her. She survived but was never the same. With the disappearance of Mori-san's wife, the rumors had started up again. Maybe it was actually the forty-year-old son who murdered her when he found she had thrown away his favorite *Shonen Jump* magazine? And was it really possible for the frail Old Mori-san to tie the complicated knots needed to keep the monster secure? Was the old man next? And then how long before the crazy son came down into the town?

Mother didn't give a straight answer. "Just don't go in. Help him open the door and that'll be enough."

Retrieving her purse from behind the bar, Hina noticed the small blue light flashing on her cell phone. Two text messages—one from Mariko and one from Tai-chan. She read each and sighed. Both mails, in sixty characters or less, were pleading their case for her virginity. *Run, run*, she thought. *You have to escape.*

Hina looked up in time to watch her mother mash a pickled plum into a fresh glass of cheap *shouchu* and lick the sour red juice from her fingers before flicking the seed onto the floor. With one hand lightly massaging the small of her back, the fat woman took the glass and waddled on her two bum knees straight past the kitchen and to the stairs that lead to their apartment above.

"Just make sure he gets inside all right. Thanks." The girl's mother did not look back, say goodnight, or even wish her youngest daughter a happy sixteenth birthday. *Didn't matter*, Hina thought, *it was past midnight anyways.*

"No problem." Hina looped her purse around her neck and pulled Mori-san's arm over her shoulder. Removing the bowl she said, "Let's get you home, okay?"

"I don't want to go home," the old man mumbled as he stood.

"You and me both," Hina said.

Old Mori-san's house was a thirty minute walk from downtown, but Hina didn't mind. She enjoyed how the rowdy narrow streets grew into wide, winding roads as all the buildings and streetlamps fell away to reveal the dark wet squares of rice fields all chattering with a thousand tiny unseen frogs. Besides, she needed time to dream up a decent excuse to tell her friends.

The road began to incline as they reached the foothills of Takamori Mountain and they were soon surrounded by clipped tea bushes in neat rows and then, higher up, by the unkempt *mikan* orchards that disappeared into pitch black forest.

The park was a flat place carved into the side of the mountain years before Hina was born. Back then the *mikan* and tea farmers all lived near their work in small homemade huts. Children were forbidden to play among the crops, so when not plucking scratchy tea leaves or tossing tiny oranges into their woven back baskets they would climb higher and deeper into the forest to engage in games of hide-and-seek and tag, romping in the streams and caves.

And then one day they began to disappear.

Whispers and rumors started as the very elderly reminisced about their own childhoods and how a mountain witch had swooped in and terrorized the villagers. She's back, they all agreed.

Most of the townspeople were too poor to desert their livelihood and relocate further down in town—although a few who actually lost children did. So on the advice of the local Shinto priest, it was decided they would instead build a small shrine to appease the bloodthirsty ogress. They also had to find a way to cease tempting her with the juicy-plump children darting in and out of her tree-shadowed forest, laughing and squealing like so many piglets.

When they reached the flat of the playground Hina gasped. Of the six lights surrounding the old park only four were standing, and only two of those working. But she could see well enough. The farthest rusted lightpost threw a long, tangled shadow across the dirt of the octopus-shaped cement slide. Hina recalled that slide painted bright red with a white towel drawn around its head and two big angry-looking eyes that were purposefully glaring at the tip of Takamori Mountain. Now the octopus was mostly just gray cement half covered in the kudzu that climbed over teeter-totters and completely engulfed the jungle gym.

The second working light stood leaning behind a bench facing the swing set. All the swings had wooden seats that had snapped in two and spent years digging deep ruts into the hard clay beneath. Hina winced at the flutter and thump as each confused and dreamy moths beat their selves repeatedly against the light, and again with the occasional clatter of the larger insects, the ones with sturdier bodies and less delicacy.

Mori-san's place was a rickety one-story house tilting curiously to the left. Behind it and all around grew the hundreds of *mikan* trees that were once Mori's prize orchard. Today they stood untended and overgrown with so many years of vegetation strangling the trunks and ladders—still in place from some long lost harvest—that it looked as if in another month the forest might finish devouring it entirely.

There were other houses still dotting the side of the mountain, all in similar states of collapse, all abandoned. However, she identified this one as the old man's abode by the single light burning in a side window. *The deranged son*, Hina thought and prayed quietly that tonight his ropes were many and tight.

Mori-san fished out his key and the girl opened the door for him and stood back.

"Are you going to be okay?" she asked.

"Fine, fine," he said kicking off his shoes and stepping up onto the hardwood floor. "Just let me get a light."

He flicked on the hallway switch, swayed. "There."

"I need to be going then," Hina said.

"Yes, you go now," Mori-san agreed, turning. "I'm home!" he called out loudly to the back of the house. Hina hurried to the park, not wanting to hear a reply if it came. She was relieved when she caught the click of the front door being shut.

Mari was right: there was no money to send her to college, not even the community one down the road. She would get older, inherit the bar, and even if she didn't gain weight she would spend the rest of her life tied to customers who were either unhappy and complaining or worse, entirely content with their lives no matter how small and mundane.

Maybe this was her chance to change her life, realign her stars. She had two choices. She could stop holding back with Tai-chan. She really did love him. And ramen shop or not, it was the most popular one in town with a solid reputation and surely making enough money for them to take occasional vacations to Okinawa and Hokkaido.

Or she could squelch any moral she ever thought she had for the next few years and work with Mari to make the big bucks.

Money she could use to get out of town, go to college, build a whole new life.

Passing through the park Hina got an idea. Brushing away as many flaking paint chips as she could, she settled carefully onto the warping wooden bench and took her mobile phone from her purse. Just as she had expected, three missed calls. The girl took a deep breath and decided she would leave her future up to fate. She typed: *Finished. Let's do it! Where should we meet?*

Before hitting send Hina glanced around the park once more and then up at the sugar-thrown sky. In her entire life she had never seen so many stars. Still prickling from hyperawareness she believed she could see them move, fleeing across the black sky, as if they were running from something just beyond the horizon.

Hina pressed the send button and smiled as a giddy burst of excitement fired in her chest. She'd sent identical messages to Mariko and Tai-chan. She would go to the first one who answered and wouldn't look back. She didn't have to choose or take the responsibility for it. She'd make the best of whatever came her way.

"Now, that was easy," she said to herself.

"Easier than you think." The growly voice came just as a gust of wind ruffled the trees and creaked the rusted chain-linked swings. It began high above and behind her, quickly swooping down until the girl felt a putrid breath tickle her ear and a laugh that raised goose flesh over her entire body. Hina startled so violently that her cell phone flew from her hand and skidded to a stop near a drying tuft of weeds several feet away. She closed her eyes until she felt the chill of the creature recede. There was the heavy sound of cloth moving and the distinct clomp of wooden *geta*-shoes digging into the soft earth. It stopped.

"I can wait all night," the voice came again, this time in front of her.

Hina opened her eyes. She knew what she'd see standing there, but still she was not prepared.

While some of her height was due to the tall three-toothed lacquered shoes, even without them the haggard old woman would have towered above any man Hina had ever met. She wore the layered silk kimono of a high courtesan complete with a wide embroidered obi tied in the front. Two hundred years ago it would have been stunning, but now it hung soiled and tattered off the woman's long-limbed frame. Even the crone's once magnificent chignon, still decorated with amber-colored pins and tortoise shell combs, was now toppling, black and white strands of waxed hair snaking down to her waist or twisting out around her head. The beast's lips were a black line pulled from one ear to the other. When she smiled her mouth fell open, dark and gaping and reeking of rot.

"Don't worry," she said. "I've been snacking. You're safe." The witch worried something from under a long fingernail and dropped it onto her leathery tongue. "For the time being, anyway."

Hina pushed back against the bench, feeling the flaking peels of paint give way and crumble beneath her, lightly showering the ground. She noticed too that all the insects so valiantly throwing themselves against their own miniature sun had vanished.

"You're Hina, aren't you?" The creature stood at an awkward angle, all her weight on one foot while the other jutted out from beneath the kimono fully exposing her thin, sinewy leg from the knee down. Hina couldn't help but glance at the bare foot, long toes split by a rich brocade strap before they curled over the high *koma-geta*. Toenails all black.

"Yes," she said. "How do you know my name?"

"I'm from around these parts. I know just about everybody." The witch reached into a fold of her obi and retrieved a *kiseru* pipe as long as her forearm. She placed it between the corner of the black slash that was her mouth and proceeded to pull out a tobacco pouch.

"I know you, your mother, your grandmother," she said, working the opposite corner of her mouth.

"My sister Kotone, too?" Hina asked.

The old woman laughed like a pile of autumn leaves on fire and Hina could physically sense the animals and insects retreating farther into the forest beyond. The silence was enormous. Shuddering to herself, Hina suspected the beast's joints were not entirely connected to one another as she threw her head back

and shifted awkwardly under her kimono. The girl stole a sideways look at Mori-san's house. Maybe the noise would wake him
up; maybe he would free his lunatic son to save her.

The crone regained her composure, rolled a pinch of shredded tobacco between her thumb and forefinger, and pushed it
into the tiny bowl of the pipe. Returning the pouch between two
layers of silk, she removed a disposable lighter from one of the
billowing sleeves of her garment, held it up to the golden lamplight and shook it beside her ear as if to check how much gas
remained.

"I travel quite a bit." She turned her head on its too-long neck
to indicate the mountains beyond. "I make my way to these parts
every ten years or so. Last time I was here you were a tiny little
thing, seemed you enjoyed playing on that as I recall." Her head
swiveled again, this time in the opposite direction looking over
her other shoulder at the octopus-shaped slide.

"You . . . ," Hina choked, ". . . were here?"

"Watching," she said, holding the flame over the bowl and
inhaling. "I'm always watching. I know just about everything
about the people in these parts, back many generations. I know
all about you."

"What did you mean, 'Easier than you think?'"

Again the old woman let loose her crackly laugh as smoke
bellowed from her mouth and nose. For an instant the air smelt
nutty-sweet and of deep earth and Hina didn't even care if this
was the end.

"First let me tell you of fate and luck and how they are measured into your blood before you are even born." The witch's
papery lips clamped around the silver mouthpiece again as she
took another long draw. "If that was it everything would be sim-
pler. But it isn't.

"There is also the residue of temperament and reason, which
parents impart upon their children. Living just a little while sees
this mixture stirred and their destinies decided. Now keep in
mind that some mixtures are pure poison." The witch's heavy
lids sagged as if suddenly tired. Gray wisps of smoke escaped
her mouth and snaked up the strands of hair fixed with thick-
toothed combs and onto the oiled locks that twisted and stood

on end around her head. "Either way almost no one realizes this fact, ignorant they can do nothing to change the direction of their lives."

"I don't understand what that has to do with . . ."

"Here, let me tell you a story," the mountain ogress began, settling deeper into her bones, sending roots shooting through the hard packed soil.

"Some tales repeat themselves over and over. This one has gone back for generations. I'll retell the most recent version. Once upon a time, there lived a young girl of extraordinary beauty but little good sense. I'll call her Hana. At a very young age Hana married the wealthiest man in town. She was sure that he would bring her happiness. However, the girl discovered that her new husband was cruel and miserly and would flee her and her only daughter the first chance he got. Let's call the daughter Kotone. Now Kotone was just as beautiful and just as dim as her mother. She loved her father and forgave him everything. She simply wanted him back, didn't understand that life was better without him. When Kotone reached an age not older than you are now, she grew sullen and distracted. Her mother, Hana, grew fat and feigned morning sickness. Conveniently, an aunt, whom no one had ever heard mentioned before, fell ill and needed assistance. Kotone was sent away only to return many months later, miraculously on the same day her mother gave birth to a baby girl. The father of this child was also of dubious character. He did not stay around. It was only a matter of time before the new child longed for her father, before she forgave him everything. They named the new child Hina."

"What are you saying?" Hina felt the roar in her blood. The surrounding trees and mountains fell away until there was only her and the truth. "That Kotone is my . . ."

"It makes sense doesn't it?"

The girl shook her head doing the simple math over and over. "They told me my father died in a fishing accident. A storm came up."

"After her father left, Kotone spent a lot of time up here at this park. She came after school. Her favorite was the slide, too."

The mountain witch pressed another ball of tobacco into the pipe and lit it. "She found quite a bit of solace in there." The crone used the end of her *kiseru* to indicate which house she was talking about.

"Mori-san?" Hina asked. "He's my . . . ?" Hina thought she was going to be sick.

"Your grandfather, actually."

This time the entire ground gave way and the girl was falling, flying. She felt the rush of waves around her ears and panic clawing up her throat.

"That crazy man who lives there, his son, he's my father?"

"Yes," the witch said.

Just then her cell phone vibrated in the dirt, its blue light blinking.

"Go ahead. Your fate is calling."

Hina wondered briefly if it was Mari or Tai on the other end. She didn't care, she wanted to run to them, either of them. *Run, run!*

"It doesn't matter really. The blood that runs through you has been the same for generations. I've seen it so many times before." The witch seemed to have suddenly lost interest in the girl. She tapped out the ash of her pipe and tucked it back inside her kimono. Pulling her leg back in, she stood up straight to her full and impressive height, her bones popping in response.

Hina stared at the phone.

"Go ahead, you had better get going," the beast said. "I believe I've worked up an appetite."

As the ogress backed away, the girl slid off the bench and retrieved her phone. She turned it over to see who had just called and then looked up at the old crone.

"I suppose I've got something to do tonight." Hina bowed her head to show respect. "May I ask something? A favor?" The hag smiled so wide that her face seemed to split in half.

"Could you take care of that for me?" Hina pointed to Mori-san's house. "Both of them."

"My pleasure." The witch made to leave, but then she stopped and asked, "What is it you have to do then?"

Hina turned off the phone and stuffed it into her purse. "I've got a kitchen to clean."

"Very good," the crone said and made her way in long heavy strides to the house with the light still burning in the window.

Hina walked over to the slide. The only remaining features were the two eyes atop the bulbous sea creature's head—mere outlines gazing up and over the mountain beyond. The eyebrows painted so many years ago in an angry V had completely worn away. Children no longer lived in these hills; their guardian no longer needed to keep his vigilant watch. Instead—his expression as proof—he spent every long night contemplating the sky and the deluge of stars, brilliant and all moving at such amazing speeds.

Each leg was a swoop of concrete, a steep or gentle slide, some even opening underneath to form tunnels where the little ones liked to crawl—where Hina played hide-and-seek with her friends. As did her mother before her. The girl lay back against one of the gentler slopes and rested her head among the leafy vines. She closed her eyes. The insects had returned to the trees and shadows and were amusing themselves once again in the warm halos of lamplight.

From old man Mori's house there came a sudden burst of noise, human and inhuman and ending as quick as it began. The silence that followed washed over the park and the girl and was then sucked back into the forest with such entirety that for a moment Hina found it difficult to catch her breath. When she recovered she found her body able to inhale deeper than before. And the air was made up of something perfumed and much more buoyant.

All around her bell crickets trilled the most exquisite song, a chorus of quivering silver prayers that she was beginning to understand. Hina clenched her muscles in response and looked up through shimmering rainbow tears. Above her hung part of a large maple tree branch. In two months time the star-shaped leaves would wake up in ochre and wine, gold and rust. But right now, for the time being, they remained an intricate filigree of sweet green, layered and shivering, excited to be young, behind them pinpoints upon pinpoints rubbing thin the very ceiling of the world. Hina gasped and wondered to herself when they'd break through and what would come in from the other side. In all her generations of living, it was the most beautiful thing she had ever seen.

the smallest unit of time

Cursing his bent legs and where they once took him, Old Mr. Tamura almost gave up. But the unexpected memory of sand and then grass beneath his feet was a taunt too cruel to let go. And so with a heart full of haste and fists knotted at his sides, he clamped his eyes shut and tried to suck in a chest full of air. With the effort came risk and, as familiar as one foot tripping over another down a flight of stairs, a potential mistake. The old man asked for too much and as it always was when he craved more than his share, he failed.

All of Mr. Tamura's long life, he had been conscious of the moment immediately following any one of his numerous big mistakes—eating the sweet bean cakes that had been left on the counter overnight, begging to ride on the top of the portable shrine after guzzling a half bottle of sake, and the minutes before marrying the woman who was sure to outlive him and care nothing about his dying.

In that instant he enjoyed a brief awareness. It felt as if he rose above time, everything slowed down. Tamura once discovered a book in the library and learned that the Hindus believe the smallest indivisible increment of time is called a *truti*. So small, in fact, that it would require thousands of these units to measure even the single blink of an eye. Still there was enough space in his newest "big mistake" for the old man to consider this research he had once made and conclude that what he was experiencing was most certainly a *truti*, most likely a whole string of them.

The moment came to him right after his chest grew as large as a mountain, right before it deflated so fast and completely that it cracked two ribs and his sternum—maddened coughing, spilling, falling; spasms on the hospital floor.

He remembered dusk. He was a child playing outside when a queer whistling made him look. A large white dog pulled a creaky, handmade cart up the narrow street, behind it hobbled a crippled man on his cane. The mothers stepped down from their *genkans*, into clicky wooden slippers. Children scattered.

Younger than that, Mr. Tamura cried and begged his mother not to go outside. When she went anyway, he'd shut himself up in the futon closet, burying his face in the calming smell, waiting for her to come back and laugh at him, to dry his cheeks with her sleeve. Older, he grew resentful as he watched her tuck coins into her apron and hurry out to join the small crowd that gathered, exchanging money for wet bags of short-necked clams or salty kelp.

They'd talk furious and nervous, giggling like schoolgirls with their hands over their mouths. After the last purchase was made, dumpy Itoh-san would remark that she was getting hungry and they'd all scurry home, just in time to turn their grilling fish and stir their purchases into the evening's miso soup. Meanwhile, the crippled man held his bow low until the last door slid closed. With his cane he'd prod the sleeping dog awake and the two would start again down the road, the man dragging his bad leg.

It was not the limp or the eerie, tuneless song that scared Tamura as a child. It might not even have been the terrible burns that the strange man tried to cover with a weepy-brimmed hat. Most frightening, he knew now, were all the unanswered questions and how a child's imagination turned to pure greed at every unknown.

Nao-kun was given credit for the *ofuro* story. Because it was true that there was an old-fashioned bathtub behind the abandoned Endo home, it was naturally true that many, many years ago this homeless, crippled stranger used to keep its waters boiling, hot enough to stew two or three children at once. Aimi added the part about how a boy once escaped, knocking the man into the fire he had recently stoked, and so caused the burns. The boy made it as far as the gate before a rabid white dog found the thick flesh of his thigh. But it was Mr. Tamura, seventy-eight years younger, who had given the man his nickname, *nopperabo*.

There was a crash, and he found himself lying twisted in the wreck of tubes, metal poles, and wet. Despite the scream of the machines, he could hear quite clearly the surreal whistle, the creak of the cart and the sound of gravel under a lame foot. And so it was that Tamura wasn't surprised, then, to see *nopperabo* walking across the room towards a chair that was meant for all of Tamura's visitors who never seemed to arrive.

"It would be you." The old man managed the words between his panicky panting breaths. *Ha. Ha. Ha.*

"*Gobusato shiteimasu.*" The unburned side of *nopperabo*'s face turned up into what might have once been a handsome smile. Both hands on his cane, he lowered himself in greeting.

"They'll be here soon," said Mr. Tamura, embarrassed. By the warmth between his legs, he realized he had wet himself. "Although it never seems like it, I'm pretty sure they're running down the hall as we speak." He stopped. "If they find you here . . ."

"Oh, we have time."

The old man crumpled on the linoleum shuddered violently.

"Here." With effort the stranger maneuvered his way to the floor by the bed. He yanked off a blanket and tucked it around Tamura. He took a pillow and after working his way down to one knee—his bad leg extended to his side—he lifted the old man's head and positioned it carefully.

"Is that better?" *Nopperabo*'s breath was sharp with the smell of salt and sea.

Is that better? Someone smoothed his hair.

Yes, thank you. The voice lightened, twisted an octave higher. *Is that better?* The perfume sweetened. A hand ran over his hair again.

"Is that better?" she asked.

"Yes, thank you," Tamura answered.

He lay on his father's futon unable to sleep, partly because of the August heat and partly because he was still remembering the taste of sake on his tongue, the song of the *funadama-sama* in his ear.

Early that morning the fishermen and their families had gathered at the docks. Men with dark skin, carrying bags tied with talismans climbed single file onto the flag-laden boat. The women and children stayed behind. Tamura's father squeezed his shoulder encouraging him to take the cloth *furoshiki*-wrapped bundle from his mother and follow him onboard. Tamura stood small among the fishermen, sailormen, and businessmen. He watched as they passed around tiny *ochokos*, every man taking his turn to tilt the giant bottle of sake into his neighbor's cup.

"I see you brought your eldest?" A balding man with a narrow smile looked down at Tamura.

"Yep, he's a man, you know." Tamura's father placed a glazed cup in the boy's palm, filled it to the brim with sake.

"Like this." He held his arm high.

Tamura, careful not to spill the drink, mimicked his father. This was his first time on the boat, and he wasn't sure he liked the way the wood fell away from his feet every few seconds or the sudden cracks and pops that came at random from where he couldn't tell. A Shinto priest dressed in layers of white silk chanted words the boy did not understand. The men all stood silent. *Did they hear it?* Chittering. *There.* Especially in the quiet between prayers. The boy knew exactly what it was.

"*Otosousan?*"

His father bent over. "What?"

"Do they keep crickets on this boat?" Hiro asked.

"What? No, of course not."

"But listen. I hear one. Do you think it's lost?" The boy pointed to the bow of the boat. And there it was, the unmistakable *rin-rin-rin* of an insect.

His father stood up, his hand lowered. "Men! Do you hear that?" he bellowed.

There was a moment of silence while everyone strained to listen.

"*Funadama-sama!*" someone cried.

"*Kampai!*" another yelled.

And they all drank. Tamura, too, put the glassy liquid to his lips. There was a roar, and he was lifted onto his father's shoulders. The shout of *"tairyou!"* was heard over and over. The men danced and jostled and slapped him on the legs. What Tamura had heard was the boat's spirit cry, the *funadama-sama*. Its song was a promise of fair weather and an abundant catch.

"Can't sleep?" his mother asked.

"No."

"Here." She picked up a paper fan and waved it above him. It perfumed the air with sandalwood. "Is that better?"

"Yes, thank you," Tamura said.

"I know what will cool you off," she said. "How about a ghost story?"

"Not too scary, though, right?"

His mother giggled. "No, not too scary. We don't want the man of the house losing sleep, do we?"

Yes, he was the man of the house now. Those were the last words his father had said as he carried him off the boat. That is, after he explained that they would be back in port only after the summer heat had lifted, cooled, and settled again, turning the leaves red and gold and then finally blowing them away. Look for the first cherry blossoms on the trees, he said. Then listen for the horns in the harbor.

"Have I told you the story of the *nopperabo*?"

"No, what's that?"

Mother positioned herself on one elbow, the other hand still fanning. *"Mukashi mukashi,"* she started. "Far, far away there was a neglected temple up in the hills. It was so ancient that the silver ceramic tiles slid from the roof and littered the ground in piles. The wooden floors were splintered and warped and there were gaping holes in the walls. Weeds and wild grasses grew into everything even strangling the *ojizo* statues that lined the walk.

"People whispered stories of how the temple had been left so quickly that many of the gilded Buddha statues and jeweled ornaments still remained. However, no one dared go up there to retrieve them. Not even in the light of day. You see, the grounds were said to be haunted." Hiro's mother looked around, at his sleeping siblings, and then over her shoulder. Her fan stopped briefly.

"But there was this one boy. I think his name was Kazuya. And he was just about your age, with hair like yours, and eyes too. Well, one day he and his friends were bored and, finding nothing to do, they decided to play a game of *jankenpon*. The loser had to climb up to the temple and retrieve some treasure. The boy's friends each threw out rock. Kazuya had chosen scissors."

"He lost!"

"Yes, but he was a brave boy and said he would go even after they decided he would have to leave at dusk. So just as the sun was going down, the boys gathered at the bottom of the stone steps and watched Kazuya carefully climb up and through the first gate. The last thing they saw was him turning to wave before pulling up his hood against the wind and going into the temple grounds.

"Once up there, he found that it was quite noisy, the wind rattling through the trees. It clattered old shutters, squeaked the long strips of wood peeling from the building. He crept past all the *ojizo* statues noticing that over time most had lost their heads. And he got all the way to the very front entrance of the temple before the moon slipped behind some clouds. It was suddenly pitch dark.

"The boy stood very still trying hard to see inside the old building. He called out, 'Is there anyone in there?' But there was no answer." His mother slowed her fanning, looked around the room as if nervous. "Kazuya took a deep breath and stepped inside. It was less windy in there, quieter and for a brief instant he felt safe. But then, from behind, something suddenly grabbed his shoulder! Are you looking for me? Kazuya turned to see the *nopperabo*, a creature that has no face!" Hiro pulled the thin sheet up over his head and kicked his legs. He squealed.

"Tamura-san! What have you done?" The nurse screamed as she ran past the disfigured man and his dog and fell to her knees beside the old man.

"Oh, what did you do? Does it hurt bad?" She touched him gently on the elbow and then the forehead. She puzzled momentarily at the blanket and pillow. "Does that hurt?"

The old man tried to answer but found he couldn't. Someone had their knees on his chest, working their hands up his throat.

The nurse moved quickly and carefully over him, around him, disentangling, adjusting, and repeating in whispers, *it'll be okay it'll be okay*. At one point a long tress of her hair fell across his face. He inhaled as deeply as he dared.

Something sweet burst into small flowers in the autumn chill, flying sideways. He lay on the ground next to the pond. Mina was above him, sitting on his thighs, the heels of both hands firmly on his shoulders.

"Kosan?"

"Okay, okay, I give up." He was mad. He had been standing near the water's edge with his finger pointed up, making tiny circles. An *oniyanma* dragonfly was eyeing him and just about to light. A dozen *shiokara* and *akiakane* dragonflies made their homes in cages in his room. But no one would believe this. He was wishing he had brought his net and thinking that maybe if he ran real fast he could retrieve it before it got too late. But the day was shorter than even yesterday and the sun had already started behind the trees. The clouds were lit scarlet and the trunks and limbs of the forest black.

It was then that Mina came sneaking up, teasing him. They wrestled, rolling from the soft earth to the grass. She was laughing the way he only heard her do when they were together. It wasn't until he turned belly up, breathless, when he felt the damp on his elbows and knees, that he knew he'd return home to again suffer the slap on the back of his head, the lecture. *Why do you spend so much time together if all you do is end up fighting?*

Mina's hands slipped off his shoulders onto the ground. Her hair had come loose in the scuffle and hung down, long and black, on both sides of her face. Against his back there was the earth and he could feel it as it fell away and crumbled into water, water that built itself back into land on the far side of the lake. Above him was the sugared breeze of orange *kinmokusei* blossoms blown from the trees. And through the chilly air the warm wheat-tea scent of Mina's breath on his face.

"Kiss me," she said. Her hand trembled as she pulled a strand of hair behind one ear. He thought she must be cold. From the grass came the trill of bell crickets, polished silver bubbles, razor sharp. Something lurched inside him, cresting; he let himself crash with it.

A moment later he was running home.

They were never close after that. Years went by, big chunks of time that he never even thought of Mina or where she was, what she might be doing. But then unexpectedly when he was moving files from his desk or riding his bike through the pines by the sea there would fire a jolt in his stomach and, however briefly, he would feel like he used to when he was around her. He ached. At those times he'd stop his work or his play and try to make the feeling last. It was only during those moments that he knew for sure that something valuable had been lost and that he would never feel like that again. And over and over he asked himself what possibly could have changed had he kissed her that day.

"I need to get help. Hang on." She touched his cheek, bringing him back into a room with a young nurse, a lame man, and a dog.

"She won't be back," *nopperabo* said.

"Huh? What?" Tamura had found his voice again, but when he tried to turn his head he discovered it was cemented to the floor. He could still see the burned man, though, from the corner of his eye. The image was watery and would stay that way until the old man found his hands, and the handkerchief he kept in his trouser pocket.

"We have a lot in common actually." *Nopperabo* leaned forward in his chair. "So what shall we talk about?"

"I don't know." The old man truly did not care. He wanted the creature to leave. He wanted to think. His mind was niggling over some unformed thought.

"There must be something you need to know."

And so if only to kill the childhood curiosity that lived on in him, he answered.

"The burns."

"Ah, the burns." *Nopperabo* made to touch his face and then stopped. Instead, his hand lowered and massaged his withered thigh. "Can I start a little before that?" He scrutinized the man on the floor for a long moment. "I'll keep it short."

"We were poor. But not as poor as most. Father worked in the *kamaboko* plant and I quit school to help. Mother mended fishing nets on the docks. Not long after Grandfather died, Grandmother fell ill. There was no one to take care of her so we took in a girl from the neighborhood. We didn't pay her of course. She was the middle of seven children. Just taking her in was a help to both families. That's the way it was done back then." *Nopperabo* paused and scratched the dog's head. "She helped with Grandmother and around the house and we fed and clothed her." He stopped petting the animal.

"She was three years older than me. I couldn't believe I hadn't noticed her before then." The burned man looked down at Tamura like he was seeing him for the first time. He moved, uncomfortable in his seat. "This is all a little embarrassing. Let's just say, we kept it a secret, how we felt about each other. There were whispers and promises. And I'm not completely sure that everyone didn't know. It lasted five months." His hand went back to his leg. "I came home from work one day and found her at the table crying, around her was scattered the day's mail. In her hands she held my *akagami*—the red paper. It was my call to war.

"Father hung out the *hata*-flags and all the neighbors and relatives came to visit and offer their congratulations. There were prayers chanted and ceremonies performed, *omamoris* sewn to keep me safe. And then I left. A year passed. Another." *Nopperabo* sat uneasy, unsure maybe. The old man began to count. He reached eighty-eight. Eighty-eight *truti*. He wished the stranger would hurry up.

"After I was burned they didn't think I'd live. I spent every day and night praying for death. I would tense every muscle, churning the pain up, throw myself from the bed. But I was a fool thinking pain could destroy me. It doesn't want to kill you. Where is the fun in that? At about the time I had exhausted myself with the effort, a doctor brought me the good news—I would live and I was going home soon. That was the funniest thing I'd ever heard. I laughed like a madman. They all assumed I was thrilled that they had saved me. What they didn't know is that my good humor came from the cruel irony of it all, that almost two years earlier, in the arms of a girl, I had prayed that hard to live. Just let me live. Now here I was given exactly what I had asked for." *Nopperabo* chuckled. "They sent me home.

"I thought about suicide, about getting off in another town, but I no longer had the strength. At the station they told me one of my mother's friends had seen me, recognized me by the bag I was carrying. She ran all the way home calling, 'Masahiro's home!' so by the time I made it to my block a small crowd had already gathered. Father was coming up the street still in his work clothes, heavy apron and boots. But all I could see was the girl in the middle of the road, in her bare feet." *Nopperabo* hung his head.

Mr. Tamura thought that he had never heard of anyone walking outside in anything but shoes or slippers. Even when the earthquake hit, even when the fire burned down the community center, everyone found enough time to pull on their shoes before they escaped.

"She stood there blushing, shuffling her feet, trying to hide them. She was the most beautiful thing I'd ever seen. 'Yuki-chan,' I called."

"Yuki?"

"Yes."

"My mother's name was Yuki." Tamura said.

"I know."

Nopperabo stared at the old man. "It was understood. We never talked about it."

"About what?" The old man tried again to turn his head, wished desperately he could move his head. The glaze in his eyes had turned his ghost into a mosaic of runny colors. He blinked several times. *Many countless wasted* trutis, he thought.

"I learned that Grandmother died while I was gone. Times had become more difficult and Yuki was now old enough to marry. Her family wanted her married. There was a fisherman that lived near the Aoba Temple."

"That's where we lived."

Nopperabo smiled his half-handsome smile. "I know."

"But how could she be so cruel?"

"Cruel?" *Nopperabo* sounded confused.

"Going out to meet you like that all those years. Acting as if you didn't have a past together."

"Your mother was anything but cruel," he said. "When my own father wouldn't look me in the eye she did. She was true to her promise to me. I was the one who . . ." Mr. Tamura heard the man exhale for a long time. "You see, we understood our families, our world, our futures. We understood the way it must be, and we accepted it. But that didn't mean we loved each other any less. On the contrary, sometimes love grows stronger in relation to what you sacrifice."

"Yeah, I guess so." He knew exactly what *nopperabo* meant and why he was there. Just then the tears released and before everything went dim again, he could see the burned man take up his cane and begin to gently poke the sleeping dog as if rousing him so they could leave.

In the area where his hip was shattered, Tamura felt only pressure, something similar to a young girl pinning him down. His sight had just about run out, but he could still hear quite well. A door opened and let in autumn, a whoosh then the *kinmoku-sei* brilliantly sweet in the air. What might have been the four squeaky wheels of a hospital cart coming fast down the hall was really the high-pitched cry of bell crickets in the tall grass. He felt someone near. But his eyes had gone useless. A tuneless whistle, the echoes of an un-oiled cart faded away. But he wasn't alone. His body lay on the damp, soaking his back and legs. He didn't care what his mother would say. Tamura had enough time inside his final *truti* to realize it was just about over. The last thing he thought to do was to prove the pain wrong and exit with two lungs full of air. He sucked in hard and was surprised not just at the lack of pain, or coughing, but that the air held no hospital reek of bleach or urine or sick, instead he was filled with the scent of earth and leaves gone soft with the end of autumn. And just before the very last *truti* ended, before he decided to follow its crumble from earth into water, he felt something soft touch his lips. His heart leapt one last time high in its broken chest when he heard the whisper of a wheat-tea fragrant voice.

"Kiss me."